Times of
Joy and Sorrow

A Collection of African American
Short Literature

By

F. HAYWOOD GLENN

Ambiance Publishing Company
Philadelphia, Pennsylvania

TIMES OF JOY AND SORROW

Copyright © 2016 by F. Haywood Glenn

ISBN: 978-0-9820101-5-0

ISBN: 0-9820101-5-X

Grandchildren fill a place in your heart that you never knew was empty. –

Unknown Author

DEDICATION

This collection of short stories is dedicated to my granddaughters, Shaliyah Marie Lockett and Aasiyah Denise Scott, and my one grandson, Anthony John Glenn, Jr.

It is my prayer that my grandchildren will know that there are no limits to their dreams. They were born with all that is necessary to achieve their goals. They have inherited a legacy of creativity, ambition, tenacity, and pride. If they can dream it and are willing to work hard for their dreams, there is nothing they cannot achieve.

Times of Joy and Sorrow

A Collection of Short African American Literature

TABLE OF CONTENTS

<u>TITLE</u>   **<u>PAGE</u>**

The Short Story

It is difficult to say exactly when the short story came into existence but its origins lie in humans desire to retell an experience. Many cultures pass down their oral history through storytelling. Storytellers in the West African Mende and Mali tribes are called "Griots." They are musicians and storytellers, retelling the history of the people through entertainment.

The short story has evolved over the years to an art form that is able to touch every human emotion and is only limited by the imagination of the writer.

The inspiration for my short stories can come in varied forms. It could be a tragic news report, a touching love song, or a new or interesting look at an historical event or period. Something sparks my imagination and my mind goes into the "what if?" mode. These things I ponder for some time before a story begins to emerge.

This collection of short stories is a compilation of the best of the stories that I have written to date. I wanted to put them all together in one volume and offer them to the reading public at a low cost.

Read and enjoy. Send comments to fhaywoodglenn@gmail.com.

Times of
Joy and Sorrow

CAPE COD LOVE

It's been more than fifty years since Anna has seen her beloved Taylor, though she thinks of him often. He seems to come to mind most often when the weather is warm and a gentle breeze sends the tide nimbly rolling to caress the southern shores of the Cape Cod coast. Anna reminisces of the summers of her youth. The memory that she savors the most is that of her nineteenth birthday celebration when she meets her first true love, Taylor Michaels.

It was the summer of 1950 and Anna's father Julius Scott, in one of his rare moments of generosity, allowed his only daughter to celebrate her birthday by giving a dinner party. The Scotts were second-generation African American owners of one of the largest resort inns on the island of Martha's Vineyard. Oak Bluffs Royal Inn's lavish facilities were usually reserved for the well-to-do African American guest who vacationed on the island. However, this was a very special day and the entire staff had been set to making Anna's birthday celebration a momentous event. To augment the evening's festivities, Julius sought the services of the jazz pianist Taylor Michaels, whom he had already booked to play at the inn for the entire month of July.

Everything was perfect. All of Anna's very best friends had been invited and with only a few exceptions, they were all in attendance. They feasted on grilled lobster tails and fillet mignon steak, clam chowder, seafood gumbo and a variety of salads and French breads. The merriment went on late into the evening.

When at last Anna stood at the door to bid her departing guests farewell and thank them for sharing in her celebration, she thought it only courteous that she personally thanked Mr. Michaels for his services. "Thank you very much Mr. Michaels. You are truly a gifted musician," she said demurely.

He stood at the door, tall and slim in his crumpled linen suit. His complexion was as dark and smooth as milk chocolate. "It's been my pleasure Miss Scott," he said as he took Anna's hand and brought it gently to his lips. Anna shivered a little at his touch and was unable to stifle the little gasp that escaped her lips. She looked down as if she expected to see the imprint of his lips on her tiny brown hand. Time seemed to stop. Anna's sudden attraction to the young piano player rendered her momentarily speechless and the moment became very awkward for the naïve young woman.

"Is something wrong Miss Scott?" Taylor asked.

Anna thought Taylor's voice was as velvety as the melodies that came from his piano. She gazed up at Taylor dreamily thinking that he was the most handsome man she'd ever seen. "No, no," she said through her embarrassment. "I think I just need some fresh air."

"Would you like to take a walk on the beach?"

Anna agreed and the two walked hand and hand down the beach. After their walk, they sat together on the pier and talked nearly the entire night. Anna listened with rapt attention as Taylor told story after story of his experiences playing behind the great Jazz singers of that time like Dinah Washington, Billy Holiday, and even Nat King Cole. Anna thought Taylor was the most exciting person she'd ever met. When dawn was finally breaking across the cape Anna became anxious. She knew that if her father were to catch her sneaking into the inn in the wee hours of the morning there would be hell to pay. They walked together back to the Inn but Taylor entered by the front door while Anna quietly slipped through the back door.

That night was the first of many, as the two began to meet more often and in secret places around the island. Taylor expressed his desire to ask Julius for permission to court his daughter but Anna warned against that idea. She knew her father well and knew that Julius would never allow her to see a musician as he had often made clear his opinion that musicians, especially jazz musicians were of the bohemian nature. The young men that her father would approve wore their oxford shirts completely buttoned and their red striped ties tightened like a little noose around their tiny necks. They wore loafers and always said, "Yes ma'am," and "yes sir." Of course, her father could not know that these same respectable young men from the very best African American families on the island were the same young men that Anna had sometimes had to fight off in the back seat of their daddy's Chevrolet on the way back from a drive-in movie.

Taylor was exactly the kind of man that Julius feared. Taylor was cool and suave, not like the stiff perfectly mannered young men with whom she had grown up. Everything about Taylor was exciting. He used words like hip, jive and solid. Even the way he walked was cool. He didn't exactly stroll it was more like a natural swagger. The fact that Taylor was fifteen years Anna's senior would of course be another point of contention had Julius known of his daughter's relationship with the piano player. The young lovers decided that it would be best not to make their relationship known at that time.

To that, point Anna had been a dutiful, well-disciplined young lady but Taylor brought excitement to her life. He was able to smuggled large bouquets of flowers into her room right under the noses of her father and the house staff. Every bouquet was always accompanied by a love note. He wrote heartfelt poetry and songs expressing his love for the naive young lady who had captured his heart.

Anna treasured Taylor's love notes. She read them again and again before hiding them away in one of her hat boxes.

After the evening meal, Anna and Julius usually spent an hour or two in the family room where Anna would read or embroider while her father talked about his famous guests and other aspects of running the inn. After Anna began to see Taylor secretly, she learned how to feign tiredness in order to be excused on the pretense that she would retire early. Julius did not know that Anna would sneak out of the back of the Inn to rendezvous with her beloved Taylor.

Anna was so in love with Taylor that had he asked her to leave everything she had ever known to go away with him; she would have gone without reservation or regret. However, Taylor had no such notions. What he eventually asked Anna was to prove her love for him and Anna, in all of her innocent naiveté, gave herself completely and unselfishly to the love of her life.

Julius, a very astute man, began to notice subtle changes in his daughter's behavior. He would catch her day dreaming at the breakfast table or sometimes even in the middle of a conversation. She hardly noticed her two Lhasa's who jumped and yelped for her attention. Julius knew that his daughter's attention was riveted on something unknown to him and he began to worry and to watch her more closely.

"Don't worry Mr. Scott," said Miss Betty his head housekeeper for the past ten years, when he had confided his worries to her one morning. "A girl Anna's age has probably got a young man on her mind."

"I figured as much but I don't understand why Anna wouldn't bring the young man home for me to meet," he questioned.

That night when Anna returned from her secret meeting with Taylor, she quietly entered through the back door of the Inn and began to ascend the stairs when she heard the booming voice of her father. "Anna!"

"Yes sir."

"Where have you been?" he demanded.

"I've been to see a friend."

"At this hour? Don't lie to me Anna. I know that you've been seeing a young man and I demand to know who this boy is!"

Anna immediately broke under her father's scrutiny. She confessed everything. She even confessed that she had not seen her monthly at its usual time and was now nearly six weeks late.

Julius was furious. "How could you do such a thing? Have you learned nothing from all my lectures and scolding?"

"I love him Daddy," was all Anna could say.

"Does he love you?"

"Yes. I know he loves me; he tells me so all of the time."

"Did he also tell you that he has a wife and two children in Boston?"

Anna felt as if she'd been run over by a truck. Every muscle in her body seemed to lose its structure and she crumbled like a deck of cards, falling on the floor at her father's feet.

Anna didn't know how long she'd been unconscious. She awoke to find Miss Betty attending her in her own bedroom. "Where is my father?" she wanted to know.

"He's gone to see your young man. He found out that Mr. Michaels had a rented room further up the coast and he's gone to confront him over your condition."

"He's going to hurt Taylor! I've got to stop him."

"Why would you think such a thing? Mr. Scott is not a violent man. He's just going to do what any father should do under the circumstances."

Anna didn't want to hear what Miss Betty had to say. She knew her father better than anyone else in the world and she knew that he would certainly want to do Taylor harm. She dressed as fast as she could and left the Inn from the front door running all the way to the Inn where she and Taylor had rented room under the names Mr. and Mrs. Michaels.

By the time she reached the Inn, she was gasping for breath.

A taxi was parked at the entrance and Anna immediately recognized the luggage tied on top of the taxi as belonging to Taylor. Her father's car was pulled into the curb behind the taxi and Julius stood leaning on the car. Anna ran to her father. "Where's Taylor?"

Taylor appeared in the doorway of the inn carrying a small valise. Their eyes met briefly, and Anna saw her own reflection fall to pieces in his eyes and she knew. He hadn't said a word but Anna knew that she had meant nothing more to Taylor than a summer fling. Julius had no need to threaten Taylor, as his intention was to leave all along. "No," Anna whispered at first. Then she screamed it as loud as she could, "No, no!"

"I'm sorry Anna," was all Taylor said before he got into the taxi and instructed the cabbie forward.

Numb with grief and humiliation, Anna continued to scream, "No Taylor! Don't go, please you can't leave now!" Somewhere in the back of her mind, she heard her father calling after her but it was too late. She couldn't allow Taylor to toss her aside, as if she were no more than a bag of dirty laundry. She had to stop him from leaving. Before anyone knew what was happening Anna ran into the path of the taxi waving her arms for the driver to stop but he saw her too late. The tires and the brakes of the taxi screeched to a halt but not before hitting Anna and flinging her tiny body across the road. As she laid there on the road with her legs twisted at an unnatural angle, she opened her eyes and thought she saw Taylor's beautiful smiling face looking down at her and she smiled back at him before closing her eyes again.

When she opened them the next time she was in her own room at the Inn. Taylor Michaels was gone. There was no trace of him. No love letters, no bouquets of flowers, no remnants of their relationship were there to remind Anna of her ordeal. In her haze, Taylor Michaels seemed to be no more than a pleasant dream.

Anna is seventy-two years old now. That day in late September 1950, Anna lost the full use of her legs and the child she thought had been conceived in love. She never heard from Taylor Michaels again. At first, she followed his career in entertainment news and tabloids but he wasn't the brilliant pianist he'd lead her to believe. He and his career eventually faded from the jazz scene.

Five years after the accident, Anna married Curtis Burton, a young man that she'd met while a student at Howard University. Ironically, Curtis was one of those young men with the oxford shirts and the tight traditional tie and Julius accepted him from their first meeting. Curtis and Anna raised a family of two daughters and one son in Boston where Curtis ran a thriving law practice. After her children had grown up and moved on to lives of their own, Anna's husband passed quietly in his sleep one evening in December 1990 and Anna moved back to her home on the Island of Martha's Vineyard.

Anna spends a lot time on the porch at Oak Bluff's Regal Inn watching the young people frolic in the sun and sand. Despite her accident, Anna was able to lead a full and happy life. The misfortune of her first love did not leave her bitter as some might expect. In fact, she hardly remembers the accident at all. What she still treasures to this day are the glorious memories of that summer in 1950 and her first taste of love.

WYATT HOUSE

Jessie was restless this morning. It was one of the first warm days at the end of the winter of 1900 so it could have been a touch of spring fever. The mansion was stuffy from being shut up all winter and as soon as the sun was high in the sky, Annie opened the French windows of the drawing room. Unusually warm March air surged through the lower floor of the house with a promise of the coming spring. Whatever the reason, Jessie just couldn't keep her mind on her chores. She should have been helping Aunt Annie polish the silver but try as she may, she could hardly keep her mind from wondering. She was thinking of the others at Wyatt House. She could remember when each of them came but it seemed that she had been at Wyatt House all of her life. She didn't remember arriving or ever being in another house. The others had all come from somewhere else, another house, and a different family.

"Jessie!" Aunt Annie startled her back to the present. "Are you daydreaming again, child? I don't have time for your foolishness today. There is so much to do before Mrs. Wyatt returns so stop that daydreaming and get back to polishing the silver."

"Yes Ma'am," Jessie said as she ducked her head down and tried to concentrate on polishing the silver flatware. However, within a few minutes, her mind began to wonder again and her thoughts moved through space and time, remembering, contemplating, and questioning. She remembered that Michael, age 16, and Henry, age 14, had come to Wyatt House in 1897 after both of their parents died from a Cholera outbreak. Laura, who was seventeen now, had run away from an alcoholic mother and should be leaving soon.

Wyatt House was not an orphanage as its few neighbors might have suspected but had the good taste not to ask. It was the home of Mrs. Victoria Whitaker Wyatt, one of Philadelphia's most prominent citizens. It was rumored that her linage went all the way back to William Penn. Victoria met Robert Wyatt while they were both students at Pinegrove University. They fell in love and were married in a very short time. Victoria was sure it was love at first sight. The Wyatt family owned considerable shares in the Pennsylvania Railroad and Robert was a wealthy man even before he graduated from the university and took Victoria as his wife.

The couple lived alone in the twelve bedroom Victorian mansion for ten years before Robert left his young barren wife and filed for divorce. Rumor and innuendo filled the society pages of the local newspapers as many suspected that Victoria's inability to conceive a Wyatt heir was the reason for her failed marriage. However, Robert married again soon after the divorce and the new wife conceived almost immediately. This prompted the gossips to believe that it was he who had been unfaithful.

Before the children came Victoria was alone in the mansion save for Annie. The two women's relationship was more than employer and employee and they had spent of lifetime of supporting each other during difficult times.

Annie Brown was the daughter of the Whitaker's cook, Mary. Victoria and Annie met when Mary would sometimes bring her daughter to work with her. The girls were around the same age and quickly became fast friends. The fact that Annie was black made little difference to the Whitakers, as they were just happy for Victoria to have someone to play with that was her own age. As the girls grew older, Mrs. Whitaker eventually hired Annie as a paid companion. Annie spent at least three days a week, some weekends, and even a couple of weeks during the summer with the Whitakers until Victoria went away to college. There was never any misconception concerning their different stations in life. Each girl accepted the other for who she was and gave little thought to anything outside of the fact that the girls simply liked each other. After being away at college for four years, Victoria missed her childhood friend dearly and once she was married, she contacted Annie and offered her a position as Household Manager. Annie gratefully accepted.

Jessie may have remembered when the other children came but she had no knowledge of how they came. Michael and Henry's parents belonged to the same church as Annie. When their Pastor heard of the parent's deaths and that the boy would be sent to an orphanage and most likely separated, he appealed to his congregation for help. Because Annie did not have children of her own or even her own home, she did not even consider taking in the boys. She casually mentioned the situation to Victoria and to her surprise; Victoria didn't bat an eye before accepting. It might be more accurate to say that Victoria allowed Annie to accept the boys. The boys would live, work, and be educated on the estate under Annie's charge. Victoria hired a tutor, Mr. Wilson, a graduate student who would teach the children reading, writing, and arithmetic three days a week. Laura came that same year. Annie would teach Laura everything she knew about managing a large estate in the hope that she would find suitable employment after her eighteenth birthday.

Jessie knew that Annie wasn't really her aunt because they all called her Aunt Annie. Once when she was just eight years old, she asked Annie about her own parents. "Where are my parents, Aunt Annie? Are they dead or did they just not want me?"

Annie had enveloped the girl in her ample arms and gently squeezed her with love. "No sweetheart, your parents are very much alive and they love you very much."

"Then why do I never hear from them? They don't come to visit or even send me a card."

"Jessica, I know that you have many questions but unfortunately there are no answers at this time. It is all so complicated. Believe me when I tell you that being here with me and the other children was the best thing your parents could do for you. When you are older all of your questions will be answered."

Annie's heartfelt explanation hardly answered Jessie's questions but it silenced her for the moment. It had been three years since Jessie had asked Annie about her parents but today, for reasons she could not explain, Jessie again wanted to know about her parents. However, this time she did not ask Annie any questions. At eleven years old, Jessie thought that she could figure it out for herself.

When all the silver had been polished to a high shine and the rest of the house was as clean as could be, Anne sent Jessie to get Michael from the garage and Henry from the stables for supper. Laura was already in the kitchen with Elsie, the cook. The aroma of roasted duck and potatoes filled the spacious kitchen. Annie and Elsie chatted as the girls began to set the table. The boys came in with James, the Wyatt chauffeur.

James was also a carpenter and had been at Wyatt House since Robert and Victoria bought the estate almost fifteen years ago. He spent his time fixing things around the estate and teaching the boys when he wasn't needed to drive Victoria. James went home some weekends but he spent a good deal of his time on the estate. He was a very tall and dignified black man with quiet demeanor and a warm smile. Everyone liked him very much, especially the boys. He sometimes accompanied Annie and the children to church on Sunday mornings.

The children and all of the house staff took their meals in the kitchen while Victoria at alone in the large dining room. This evening, Victoria was unusually late. For reasons no one knew, a car had come for her early that morning. She hadn't told Annie where she was going. Annie, not wanting to take advantage of their peculiar relationship, never pried.

The kitchen was buzzing with chatter as everyone sat down to eat. Jessie poured lemonade in each of the glasses and Laura brought a basket of fresh rolls to the table. Once everyone was seated, Annie began the blessing. "Our Father, who art in Heaven, give us this day . . . ."

Victoria rarely visited the kitchen that is why her sudden appearance at the kitchen door startled everyone. She pushed open the door and stood for a moment in the doorway. Her eyes scanned the faces of the group but lingered for a second on Jessie. Then she quickly turned her attention to Annie. "Annie, forgive me for interrupting your meal but it is urgent that I to speak with you for a moment." Annie immediately left the table.

"Shall I get your supper now?" Elsie asked.

"No. Finish your meal then I'll take supper in my room."

"Yes Ma'am," Elsie whispered.

Annie and Victoria left the room and Annie did not return for nearly an hour. Only Elsie who had delivered a supper tray to Victoria's room and saw the fragile condition of her mistress. "My, she looked so weak. Did she tell you if she were ill?" Elsie asked Annie.

Annie did not answer until they were alone in the kitchen. "Yes, she is ill but she has been for quite some time. The doctors have given her only a few months to live but apparently her mother took her to see a different kind of doctor, hoping for some miracle cure."

"What is it? What illness does she have?" Elsie questioned.

"I'm not really sure. It has something to do with her blood."

"And there is no cure?"

"No cure." Annie confirmed.

The next couple of weeks went on as usual in the Wyatt House save for the comings and goings of family and friends who came to visit with Victoria who never left a room again. To everyone's surprise, even Robert came for a visit.

It was on April 13, 1900, Jessie's twelfth birthday, that Victoria requested to see Jessie. Holding tight to Annie's hand, they entered Victoria's bedroom. Victoria lay propped upon several pillows. Her skin was sallow and her hair was disheveled. "Victoria," Annie whispered.

Victoria opened her eyes and Jessie was sure she saw tear streaks on her pale cheeks. "Hello, Jessica." she said.

"Hello."

"Today is your birthday, isn't it?"

"Yes, Ma'am."

"Well, Annie tells me that you are a bright student."

"Yes, Ma'am," Jessie said again.

"I want to give you a birthday present," Victoria said in a weak voice. She went into the night table drawer, came out with a gold chain with a tiny gold cross, and handed it to Jessie.

"Thank you," Jessie said not hiding her surprise.

"You are welcome," Victoria said. She motioned to Jessie to come closer and Jessie took one small step closer to the bed. "You are a very special girl, Jessica, and you have a bright future ahead of you. I want you to remember to always be kind to others and the world will be kind to you in turn. Do you understand?"

"Yes, Ma'am," Jessie said though she was more puzzled than ever.

"Goodnight, Jessie."

"Goodnight Miss Victoria."

Once Annie and Jessie were in the corridor, Jessie said, "What was that about?"

"I think she just wanted you to know that she thinks that you are a very special girl, just like she said." That explanation was good enough for Jessie and she thought no more of their conversation.

That night Victoria passed away in her sleep. The undertaker came to dress the body and prepare it for the wake. Victoria was dressed in a beautiful white gown and slippers. Her beautiful red hair was piled on top of her head and pinned with little satin daisies and sprigs of baby's breath. Her lips were covered in a muted shade of pink, which clashed with the brightness of her hair. The coffin was set up in the parlor and surrounded by every possible variety of flower arrangements.

The house staff and the children most always used the side and back doors to come and go but the children now took special care not to go near the parlor. They were all sad at

Victoria's death but not distraught as they barely knew their
benefactor and rarely saw her as they went about their daily
activities. Annie was the only one who truly knew Victoria and
her grief was profound.

On the day of the wake, the children were dressed in
their best and sat on the front row of the parlor. James and Elsie
sat on the back row. James seemed especially upset and wore
sunglasses, even inside the house.

Jessie sat beside Annie who was distraught and let her
tears flow freely. Eventually, Jessie began to cry too, though it
was more for Annie's grief than the mourning of Victoria. A
minister from the Presbyterian Church came to give the eulogy.
When the wake was over, all the people filed into the foyer and
dining room except James. When everyone else had gone, he
closed the doors and moved closer to the coffin. He took off his
glasses and stared down at Victoria. "I would have done
anything to save you Vickie. I still love you with all my heart
and I will cherish your memory and the memory of us," he said.
He thought he was alone but Jessie watched from behind the
heavy drapes.

The day was long and tiresome and everyone was glad
when it was over. When the last person finally left the house,
Elsie and Annie went about putting the house back in order and
cleaning the kitchen. Michael was the first to drift into the
kitchen soon followed by Henry and Jessie.

"Aunt Annie," he whispered. "What is to happen to us
now? Will we be sent to an orphanage?"

Annie knew that there would be questions but she
didn't think they would come so soon. "Honey, the truth is I
just don't know, but I do know Mrs. Wyatt. I know that she was
a thoughtful and generous woman and I'm sure she made plans
for each of you. We will just have to wait for the reading of the
will, which should be in a week."

That week was the longest the children ever knew.
Michael and Henry worried that they would be split apart and
Jessie feared the unknown. Annie was all she knew and she
couldn't imagine living with anyone else.

Finally, it was the day of the reading of the will.
Besides her attorneys, Victoria's parents, her sister, and Robert
came and shut themselves in the library for more than an hour.
Finally, the attorney called for Annie and Jessie.

"Me?" Jessie questioned. "Why me?" The others
looked from one to the other but none of them could answer her
question.

Annie and Jessie quietly entered the library amid the
stares of Victoria's family and the snicker of Robert, her ex-
husband. "Ah, Miss Brown," the attorney, Mr. Harris said.
"Have a seat." Annie and Jessie took seats close to the desk. "It
seems that Victoria was more than a little fond of you, Annie.
She left you a sizeable amount of money and a request that the
new owner allow you to reside at Wyatt House for the rest of
your life."

Annie's mouth opened as if to speak but found that she
had no voice. She was, in fact, speechless. She turned to look at
Mrs. Whitaker, who simply smiled and nodded her head.
"Thank you," was all she could think to say.

"As Executor of Victoria's will, I will be by later this
week with paperwork that requires your signature."

"Yes, sir," Annie said.

The attorney then turned his attention to Jessie. "Well,
young lady. I dare say, you are about the luckiest Negro in
America." Jessie frowned. It was at this point that Robert rose
and stormed from the library, letting the door slam loudly
behind him.

"Let us begin at the beginning. First, your name is not
Jessica Brown, as I'm sure you have been told. Your real name

is Jessica Ann Whitaker. Victoria was your mother. Your father is unknown save the fact that he was obviously a Negro. This house and the art gallery in the city, along with a sizable amount of money, will be held in trust for you until your twenty-first birthday or your graduation from the University of your choice, whichever comes first. Now I am pleased to introduce you to your maternal grandparents." He then extended his hand toward the Whitakers. "Mr. and Mrs. Whitaker, meet Jessica. This is the daughter that Victoria was able to keep secret for twelve years."

Like Annie, Jessie was speechless. If the Whitakers had misgivings, they gave no clue. Mrs. Whitaker, close to eighty now, had grown up in a family of abolitionist. She stepped forward to give her granddaughter a hug. "I know you are too young to understand but it was important for Victoria to keep you a secret. She could have been ruined had the knowledge of an illegitimate black child been known among her contemporaries. Now that you know the truth dear, it is up to you to keep the secret. We will say that you were adopted by Victoria."

Jessie said not a word. It was if she was in shock.

"No one will speak of your parentage once we leave this room," said Mr. Harris. "You are a wealthy young woman and as Victoria's adopted daughter there is no one who will contest the validity of her will. Do you understand?"

"Yes, I think so," Jessie answered. The meeting was over and everyone was preparing to leave when Jessie stopped them all. "Wait," she said. "What about the others?"

"The others?" Mr. Harris questioned.

"Michael, Henry, and Laura, what will happen to them?"

"What would you suggest?" Mr. Harris questioned.

Jessie was thoughtful for a moment. "Nothing," she finally said. "I want them to go on living here until they are grown up."

"As you wish, Madam," was all Mr. Harris said.

That evening as Elsie prepared supper, Jessie went to the kitchen. Annie and James were both there in the kitchen. "Aunt Annie, why do we have to eat in the kitchen?"

"We don't. That was Victoria's preference."

"But, this is my house now, right."

"Yes, but technically not until you reach eighteen."

"Well, I no longer want to eat in the kitchen. We will all eat in the dining room, if that is alright with you, Aunt Annie?"

"That is fine, Miss Jessica." Annie smiled.

That night supper was like a celebration of sorts. They were all sorry about Victoria's passing but jubilant about Jessie and Annie's good fortune.

When James excused himself to go to put the car back into the garage Jessie followed him outside. There in the courtyard, with the wind gently blowing and the sun beginning to set, she called after him. "Hey Mr. James. You know what I think?"

"No, Jessie. What do you think?"

"I think that Victoria was my mother and you are my father."

At first, he just stared at her then he shook his head. "No. What would make you think such a crazy thing?"

"I once asked Aunt Annie about my parents and she said that they were both very much alive. Victoria is gone now but the attorney made no mention of my father."

"Maybe he doesn't know your father."

"Maybe," she admitted. "But I heard you say that you loved Victoria."

At that moment, time seemed to stop. Neither moved for moment, the magnitude of what Jessie had witnessed both embarrassed and delighted James. In just two long strides, he was at her side. He dropped down to one knee and took Jessie into his arms. For a few moments, he just held her close. "I still love Victoria and I love you just as much but you must make me a promise."

"I already know what you are going to say. You want me to keep a secret. You don't want anyone to know that you are my father."

"Yes. No one can know. It could cause me more than a little trouble. That's why Victoria didn't tell anyone. You're too young to understand now but you will when you are older."

"I understand more than you think but I'll keep calling you James if you promise to never go away from Wyatt House."

"I promise."

THE EYES OF TROY

There was something familiar in his sad eyes. His unsmiling face and downcast eyes stood out from the page of brightly smiling children. My gaze lingered on his face for a moment as I wondered why I suddenly felt a connection to this child.

My wife urged me to turn to the next page but something that I could neither understand nor explain held me there. I just couldn't seem to move past the child's eyes. Big brown eyes in a lighter brown face, shaded by thick dark fanning lashes held me captive. He had the look of someone who had faced the trials of life, seeing the worst and the best of our sometimes chaotic and most times amazing world, though I knew that the boy couldn't have been more than eight or nine years old. What had he experienced in his short life that could make him so sad, I wondered.

I shifted uncomfortably in my chair as recognition crept up my spine like a winter chill. This child whom I had never met had somehow touched my soul. I was confused by my conflicting emotions, feeling exhilarated as if I'd found a hidden treasure and a moment later I felt as if I'd committed some horrible crime against humanity.

"Honey, I thought we agreed that we wanted an infant," my wife whispered.

Yes, I wanted to say but I couldn't bring myself to answer her aloud. I knew at that moment that those eyes were a window into my past and the same eyes that had haunted me for most of my adult life. The one thing that I was sure of was that I somehow knew this child. What would my wife say if she knew what I was thinking?

I pointed a nervous finger at the photo. "What's his name?" I asked Mrs. Ewing, the adoption agency social worker.

She shuffled through a handful of cards before she answered, "His name is Troy."

The look on my wife's face told me that my question had annoyed her. I knew she didn't understand. How could she understand what was happening to me when I couldn't even put it into words? I turned away from the photos trying to shake the uneasy feelings but I couldn't help wondering why I ever agreed to adopt in the first place. After all, hadn't our doctors assured us that there was no reason why Denise and I could not one day conceive a child of our own? Had it not been for Denise's impatience we would never have come through the agency's doors. After five years of marriage, Denise was desperate for a child and I agreed to adoption for no other reason than to make her happy. It all seemed perfectly normal then, but now I had the feeling that something more than coincidence had brought me here and made it possible for me to look into the eyes of Troy.

When I turned away from the window, Mrs. Ewing and Denise were pouring over an album of infants who had recently been place for adoption.

"What else can you tell me about Troy?" I interrupted.

Denise got up and walked away not bothering to hide her frustration.

"Troy is eight years old and was born in Virginia," Mrs. Ewing went on as if she were citing the merits of some new product instead of a child. "He's a good student and a fairly good artist for a boy of his age. He likes airplanes and spends a lot of time drawing airplanes. He also likes reading and skating." My mind raced back in time as she spoke and I scarcely heard a word she said.

"Is he orphaned," I asked.

"No. Troy was placed for adoption at birth. However, he has been with this agency for a little under six months."

"Can we find out who his real parents are?"

"Absolutely not," Mrs. Ewing said. "We pride ourselves on keeping our adoptions completely private and in the strictest confidence. Our clients are assured that the adoption records are sealed for twenty years or at the very least, until the child reaches adulthood."

"Why hasn't he been adopted?"

"Jordan!" my wife exclaimed. I was aware that I was upsetting Denise but still I had to know more about Troy.

"Mr. Roberts there are many reasons why a child is sometimes hard to place. It is often difficult to place African American children. There just aren't enough African American families seeking adoption. Aside from that, with no physical or mental handicaps it is impossible to know why some children are easily placed while others may be more difficult. However, in Troy's case I'd have to say that it could be that the child is rather withdrawn. He doesn't exactly endear himself to people."

"You mean that the boy is shy?"

"Well, I guess that's one way to put it."

"Troy," I repeated the name as if all of my questions would somehow be answered through the mere utterance of his name. Who was this boy whose eyes had so captivated me and why did I feel a connection with a child whom I knew that I had never seen before in my life? The connection was so real and so strong that it simply could not be ignored. Whether by fate, coincidence or something paranormal, I knew I was supposed to be here at this time for a purpose.

As I struggled with my rising anxiety, everything suddenly became as clear to me as if I'd known the truth all along. I knew this child. The dimple in his round chin, the high hairline, straight nose, and full lips were all as familiar to me as my own face. I also knew that if I turned away now I would see those hunting eyes for the rest of my life.

"Can we meet him?" I asked.

"Jordan?" Denise questioned. I got up and moved away from the desk again, leaving my wife and Mrs. Ewing to browse through the photos alone. Thrusting my restless hands deep into my pockets, I walked away from the ladies and stared out of the window. I could almost feel their questioning stares as they bore into my back before they both returned their attention to the children's photos.

Again, my mind wondered backward. I knew that Denise had her heart set on an infant and I wanted more than anything to please her, but everything I felt was changed the moment I looked into the eyes of Troy. How could I explain to Denise what I felt for this child? Those haunting brown eyes had taken me to a place I thought I would never have occasion to revisit, my youth. At that moment, I knew that I could not go on with this any longer.

"Mrs. Ewing," I interrupted again. "Would you mind leaving my wife and me alone for a few moments to discuss the adoption?"

"Certainly," she said warily.

As soon as the door was closed behind Mrs. Ewing, I went to Denise and took her in my arms. I held her close for a few moments as I tried to calm her fears. "You don't want an infant, do you Jordan?" she asked through her soft sobbing.

"No Denise, but there isn't anything for you to worry about."

"Is this about the boy?"

"Yes," I said as we sat together. "The moment I looked at him I recognized something in his eyes. I'm going to tell you a story and I just want you to listen before you make any judgments."

She nodded as she dabbed at her tear stained face with a tissue.

"Troy's eyes reminded me of a girl named Lisa that I knew in high school. She was a perky little cheerleader with those same big brown eyes. Her bubbly personality made her one of those girls that seemed to be friends with the entire school. I wasn't as popular. I was known more for my ability to slam dunk on the court than my personality. Most people in my high school thought I was arrogant and standoffish but the truth is I was just very shy. I was never the suave gamer who felt comfortable talking to girls, especially popular girls like Lisa. I was shocked when she actually talked to me one day in our school lunch room."

"Oh, get to the point Jordan," Denise snapped. "You dated her and now you think this boy is yours?"

"I wouldn't exactly say that Lisa and I dated although we did become very comfortable with one another. We spent a lot of time together over the summer between eleventh and twelfth grade and we soon became intimate. We were both so inexperienced and inept in our attempt at lovemaking that the possibility of conceiving a child never occurred to either of us. Late in September of that same year, Lisa told me that she was moving to Virginia to live with an aunt. Of course, I thought it was very strange that she would just up and move while her family stayed in Philadelphia but Lisa said that her aunt was very sick and her parents wanted her to stay with her aunt to help out. She said that she'd be back by the next summer and I never thought about it again and I never saw Lisa again. It wasn't until I looked at that photo that it all came back to me. No one had ever told me that our clumsy attempt at lovemaking had produced a son."

"Jordan, how could you possibly think that this boy is your son? You don't know anything about him."

"Intuition, a gut feeling, or anything else you'd like to call it but I know that this boy is my son and I'd like for us to adopt him."

Denise didn't say anything for a few moments and during that brief period of silence; it seemed as if the entire world had come to a stop. I didn't want to hurt Denise but after all, neither of us professed to be virgins when we married.

"Denise, you know that had I known that I had a son I would have done everything in my power to take care of him. I'm not saying that we can't adopt an infant. I'm only saying that I want to adopt Troy."

"What if he's not really your son?"

"Once we adopt him, he'll be our son."

"What about testing?"

"Absolutely, if that is what it will take to convince you that this is right?"

"You don't need convincing?"

"No, I'm surer about this than anything else in my life."

Denise just stared at me as if she thought I had lost my mind. I didn't know what else to say to her to make her believe that this was right. I was asking my wife to agree to raise a child that I had fathered with someone else. I glanced down at the photo again. "This is our son Denise," I whispered.

"I'll tell Mrs. Ewing that we've made our decision," Denise said.

Four weeks after that meeting, we brought Troy to our home. DNA test confirmed that Troy is indeed my biological son. However, as it turned out Troy wasn't the sad little boy he appeared to be in the adoption agency photo. He is a happy and active little boy and quite a handful for Denise and me.

During the first few months after adopting Troy, we were both so overwhelmed with our new responsibilities as parents, that Denise hardly ever mentioned the infant that she was so desperate to adopt. She wanted so much to be a good parent to Troy that her anxieties over his conception faded away. As fate would have it, my wife is now expecting our second child.

INITIALS OF THE ACCUSED

It was one of those Philadelphia summers when the humidity and the temperature raced to the top of the thermometer. At ten in the morning, the mercury had already climbed to an astounding ninety degrees. I decided on a tall cold glass of lemonade instead of my usual cup of black coffee. I sat down at the kitchen table to scan through the morning paper. I don't usually read the obituaries but this morning something caught my eye. "GWENDOLYN ANDREWS of the Germantown section of Philadelphia, Pennsylvania; devoted wife of Dr. Bernard Daniel Andrews; beloved mother of Jeffrey and Peter Andrews, departed this life on May 10, 1999."

I hadn't thought of the Andrews family in over thirty years. There was no way that they could have known that the few days I spent with the family back in 1969 had changed my view of the world. That isn't to say that my experience with the Andrews family was either positive or completely negative. It would be more accurate to say that I learned that people are not always, what they seem.

The Andrews were a prominent Christian family in our community and one of the few white families who hadn't moved out of the area when African Americans began to move in. Mrs. Andrews was often recognized for her charitable contributions to the needy, while Mr. Andrews boasted that he had been among the 200,000 Americans that marched on Washington with Dr. King. My grandmother had worked for the Andrews family as a maid for nearly ten years and she thought very highly of the family, especially Mrs. Andrews.

I sat back in my chair, took a long sip of the cool liquid, and let my mind carry me back to when I was a boy of fourteen years old.

My mother died when I was baby and I grew up with my father and grandmother. My father was a trucker and had gone on a long distance run to the west coast. As usual, I was left with my grandmother. However, a couple of days after my father left, my grandmother became ill and had to go into the hospital. Not knowing how long my father would be away, my grandmother wasn't comfortable with leaving me at home and on my own, for God knows how long. She expressed her concern for me when she spoke to Mrs. Andrews about her impromptu hospital stay and was greatly relieved when Mrs. Andrews offered to let me stay with her family until my father returned.

My grandmother told me to be mindful of my manners and grateful that the Andrews were such nice people to accept me as a guest in their home, and I was subsequently dropped off on the Andrews' doorstep.

I remember sitting in the dining room of the Andrews' house on Upsal Street. My hands were folded in my lap as I concentrated on being as quiet as possible. I sat motionless, my eyes focused on my folded hands. I didn't dare move for fear that I may call attention to myself by those who, I was sure had forgotten that I was even in the room. I'd been summoned to this same dark and gloomy room about the same time the day before.

"Billy," Mrs. Andrews shouted. She always shouted when she spoke to me, except of course when my grandmother was around. When she spoke to Mr. Andrews or her sons Peter and Jeffrey, her voice was soft, almost musical. She stood over me with her hands braced on her hips while I tilted my chin toward my chest and studied her slipper-clad feet. I dared not look directly at Mrs. Andrews. I knew that looking her right in the eye would only make her angrier. "Billy, I want the furniture in this room waxed and polished. Do you understand?"

I was so shocked at her order that I ventured to lift my chin just a fraction. I only wanted to get a peep at her face. I hoped to see just a hint of a smile, anything that would indicate that this was all a big joke. I was a guest in the Andrews' home, or at least that was what my grandmother was led to believe. However, there was no smile on Mrs. Andrews face and I knew at that moment that I had been stripped of my status as a "guest." Instead of the smile I sought, I encountered a smirk. I was more than puzzled because the Andrews had always seemed to be nice people. I couldn't even count the number of times I'd heard that phrase, "nice people" in reference to the Andrews.

"Don't look so surprised Billy. I think that this is the least you can do to repay my husband and me for our kindness, don't you agree?"

I didn't agree but what I said was, "Yes ma'am."

"I thought you would agree." Now she smiled but it wasn't a happy smile. It was an evil smile. I was relieved only when she turned to leave the room but I exhaled too soon because she stopped and slowly turned to face me again. "Oh, Billy, be careful not to leave even a tiny smudge or you'll be without supper tonight. Is that clear, young man?"

"Yes Ma'am," I muttered. The evil smile broadened and she walked away humming a familiar hymn.

Mrs. O'Leary was the Andrews' cook. She came in from the kitchen and handed me several pieces of cloth and the wood polish. "Mrs. Andrews doesn't mean any harm Billy. Oh, I know that she sometimes seems a bit gruff but that's just her way. She really does have a kind heart son." I didn't offer a response. I now knew that Mrs. Andrews' kind heart was reserved for certain people and I wasn't one of them. Mrs. O'Leary chattered on. "Oh and she loves children. Did you know that she used to teach

Sunday school? Yes," she answered her own question. "Almost twenty years she taught the Scriptures. Mr. and Mrs. Andrews are the kindest and most Christian people I know. You'll come to like them son, I just know you will."

I got to work quickly because, in spite of what Mrs. O'Leary thought of the Andrews', I had the feeling that Mrs. Andrews was a woman of her word. I polished the dark wood until I could see my face in the table. I had to get a ladder from the basement to reach the big china cabinet and I crawled on my belly to reach the big wood claws and legs under the table and buffet. I polished and buffed until I smelled as if I were also wooden. By the time I'd finished it was well past lunch. I heard Mrs. Andrews call her sons Peter and Jeffrey to lunch and later I heard the two of them laughing and chattering away in the big kitchen. Mrs. O'Leary came in to check my work.

"Good job. Billy you've done a very good job. I think Mrs. Andrews will be pleased. Off with you now, go and wash your hands. I've got a nice lunch waiting for you in the kitchen."

"Yes ma'am," I said. I hurried up the stairs to wash up while thinking that it wasn't so bad after all. My father and grandmother always gave me chores to do around the house and it was awfully nice of the Andrews' to allow me to stay. Polishing some furniture was a small price to pay for their kindness. Mrs. Andrews had probably given chores to her sons as well.

After washing my hands, I headed straight for the kitchen. The aroma of chicken soup filled the air and I realized that I was hungry. However, when I reached the kitchen door Mrs. Andrews stood blocking my way. "Billy," she said, "Didn't I tell you what would happen if you didn't do a good job?"

"Yes Ma'am, but . . . ."

"Now don't talk back young man. Your grandmother would be very displeased to hear that you've been disrespectful.

My husband and I were kind enough to take you into our home while your grandmother is in the hospital. We didn't have to do this, you know. Now you really don't want me to tell your grandmother that you've misbehaved, do you?"

"No Ma'am."

"Now,' Mrs. Andrews said, satisfied that she had successfully hushed my protest. " Jeffrey has brought a dreadful discovery to my attention. The initials B. D. have been carved into the wood on the bottom of my dining table. Do you have any idea how this happened?

"No!"

"What is your last name Billy?"

"Davis Mrs. Andrews, you know that but I didn't mark your table."

"Yes, of course you didn't Billy. Someone else crawled under my table and carved your initials while you were busy polishing away. Is that what you expect me to believe Billy?"

Mrs. Andrews' habit of making her point with a question was as annoying as her ridiculous accusation. "I don't know how your table got marked. I just know that I didn't do it." Peter and Jeffrey snickered behind their mother's skirt as the tongue-lashing went on for several more minutes.

"Would you believe such a story Billy? I don't think so. This table has been in my husband's family for many years and now you've ruined it. You've ruined a valuable antique and you will have to pay for your vandalism. I haven't decided just how you will pay since I'm sure that money is out of the question. So, until my husband and I have discussed this matter, you are to go to the room that you've been given and stay there until I call for you."

I didn't bother to argue. I knew that it would do no good. Mrs. Andrews had already made up her mind before she ever met me. She just didn't get it. Her husband may have marched with

Dr. King and she may help the needy but she still didn't get it. She never saw me; she only saw who she already thought I was. When it came right down to it, Mrs. Andrews was as prejudiced as any of those good old boys from the south, who rode around with a confederate flag waving from the car antenna. Mrs. Andrews was a closet red neck.

The room that I'd been banished to was a tiny room all the way at the top of the house, the attic. The ceiling was slanted so that my five foot, nine inch frame could not stand upright in the room. It was small and dusty and had been used for storage until awarded to me as my make-believe prison. I was confined to the attic the remainder of the day and that night. There was no electricity in the room and Mr. Andrews would not allow me to have a candle. As I sat in the dimly lit room, the only light coming from the fading stream of sunlight through the skylight in the ceiling, I couldn't help thinking how I would have preferred to stay in our tiny apartment until my father returned or my grandmother was home from the hospital.

I slept very little that night. My mind concocted images of what my fate would be at the hands of grandma's kindly employers. I noticed a stack of comic books and paperback novels stored in a cardboard box. The first paperback I picked up was an old Hardy Boys mystery. I thought that reading might help to pass the time. With the sunlight fading, I opened the book. On the inside cover I read, "If you steal this book you steal in shame because BERNARD DANIEL ANDREWS is not your name."

"Bernard Daniel Andrews," I said the name aloud realizing that the book must have belonged to Mr. Andrews as a boy. Mrs. Andrews did say that the table had been in the Andrews family for many years. The more I thought about it the more I was convinced that Mr. Andrews had carved those initials in the table a long time ago. He had defaced his parent's table and now

I knew it. But, how could I convince Mrs. Andrews of this when the initials under the table were B. D. If Mr. Andrews had done this carving, the initials should have been B. D. A. How could I prove my innocence?

I tossed and turned on the little cot most of the night. Sleep became more impossible with every hour. I was haunted by those initials. I needed to see them for myself. Maybe Jeffrey's word was enough for Mrs. Andrews but I needed to see the table. Maybe there would be something that would prove that I couldn't have defaced their precious antique table. Finally, I decided that I couldn't wait any longer. I tried the door.

Grateful that I had not been locked in, I slowly opened the door. I crept down the stairs and into their large dining room. My heart pounded so hard I thought I could almost hear it pulsating. The room was very dark. I parted the heavy drapes just enough for a stream of moonlight to brighten my way then I dropped to my knees and crawled under the table, running my fingers along the wood until I could feel the deep creases of the carving. I had to twist my head and an awkward angle to see just how the table had been defaced. "B. D. A., 1945," I read aloud. Just as I suspected, Mr. Andrews had carved his initials into his parent's table. I could prove that I was not guilty. Finally, I took a deep breath and the pounding in my chest began to slow as my heart rate returned to normal. I carefully closed the drapes and crept back to my small attic room. It was easy to fall asleep now.

About nine o'clock the next morning Mrs. O'Leary came to tell me that Mr. and Mrs. Andrews wanted to see me in the dining room. This is it, I thought. Mrs. O'Leary waited outside the door while I dressed. As soon as I came into the dining room, I was ordered to a chair in the corner, while Mr. and Mrs. Andrews discussed my fate as if I weren't even in the room. Dr. Andrews said very little while Mrs. Andrews went on and on about how the working class, and especially Negroes, must be taught respect for those who were blessed with wealth. Dr. Andrews paced the room with both of his hands in his pockets. Occasionally he would look at his wife and shake his head in agreement. Finally, he said, "Aren't you being a little too hard on the boy, Gwendolyn? After all, it is a very old table."

"No, I don't think so. If these people want to be treated as equals they must learn that this kind of behavior is unacceptable."

Dr. Andrews would say no more.

A short time later Mrs. O'Leary came to the door and announced that, my father had arrived. I don't ever remember being so happy to see my father as I was that morning. I suddenly didn't care about being noticed and I dashed across the room and leaped headlong into my father's arms. Being almost his height at fourteen, I nearly knocked him off of his feet. Dr. and Mrs. Andrews were both flabbergasted. They were so surprised to see my father that they had forgotten about me.

"Why, Mr. Davis," Mrs. Andrews said. "We didn't expect you so soon."

"Yes, I know. A friend contacted me on the radio and told me that my mother had taken ill shortly after I left so I just turned around and came right back as soon as I could. I want to thank you both for taking care of Billy. It was very kind of you. I hope he wasn't any trouble." My father had no idea.

I wanted to just scream out and tell him how wrong he and Grandma were about the Andrews. They may be kind on the surface but in their hearts, they were narrow minded, prejudiced people. But then, I thought, what if they tell my father about the table?

To my surprise, they said nothing.

"Well, you know how we love your mother, Bill. She's a very dear woman and we were happy that we could help in some small way," Mrs. Andrews lied. When she turned to face me, I noticed that the evil smile was gone. "Billy, hurry and get your things dear. I'm sure your father is anxious to get to the hospital."

"Yes Ma'am." When I went back to the attic room for my belongings, I took that old Hardy Boys paperback with me. I just had to let the Andrews know that I had nothing to do with defacing their precious table but for some strange reason, I suddenly had no wish to diminish them in my family's eyes. My grandmother had often remarked about how the Andrews were good Christian people and they were the perfect examples of how we could all live without prejudice. It occurred to me that maybe Mrs. Andrews didn't even know that she was prejudiced. Even so, she was wrong about me and I had to let her know that.

My father thanked the Andrews once again while we stood on their front porch and they both assured him that I had been no trouble at all.

"Mrs. Andrews," I said.

"Yes, Billy." She answered me in that musical voice that she usually reserved for her own family.

"Do you remember that wood carving you were telling me about yesterday?"

For a moment, I thought I saw that evil smile but it faded and she just looked puzzled. "Yes," she said warily. The word came out quickly as if she were in a hurry to end the conversation.

"Well, I got a closer look at it late last night. It reads B. D. A., 1945 and not just B. D. I guess Jeffrey didn't really get as good a look at it as I did." I stole a quick sidelong glance at Jeffrey who was peeping around the almost closed door.

"How very observant of you, Billy. Now run along dear. Your father is waiting."

She still didn't get it. "Good-bye Mrs. Andrews," I said.

"Good-bye Billy. It was a pleasure to have you," she lied again.

My father had already climbed into the cab of his truck and only Mrs. Andrews and I stood on her front porch. "Oh, I almost forgot." I fished the paperback from my bag. I borrowed this book from Dr. Andrews' collection in the attic." I opened the front cover so that she could see the inscription and handed it to her. "Would you please return this to Dr. Andrews?"

I watched her eyes quickly scan the writing on the inside cover of the book. "I'd be happy to return the book for you," she said but she still didn't get it.

"By the way," I said. "Dr. Andrews' first name is Bernard, isn't it?"

"Yes," she said. I could see her begin to flush as she realized how wrong she had been. She had heard Dr. King's "I Have a Dream" speech and even celebrated it but she hadn't yet learned to judge people by the content of their character. No matter how hard she denied her prejudice she had judged me on the color of my skin.

"Billy, I'm sorry, I thought . . ."

"I know what you thought Mrs. Andrews but you were wrong. I think that you are probably wrong about a lot of things and maybe even a lot of people. Don't worry, though. No one will ever know unless you tell them. Good-bye Mrs. Andrews."

We moved away the following year and I never saw any of the Andrews again. I use to wonder if Mrs. Andrews ever thought of me. More often than not, I wonder whenever I meet a person for the first time, if that person is really seeing me or just who they assume me to be.

PURPOSE AND PASSION

Coretta stretched her long arms out wide and yawned. It was still early in the day and there was no reason why she should feel so sluggish. Bored with the daily routine of her life, she had become restless and felt somewhat peculiar lately. She didn't know why she felt these things but she could hardly deny that she hadn't felt herself lately. Her mother said that she had no reason to feel out of sorts; after all, she was still a newlywed.

"Ink hasn't even dried on the marriage license yet and you already finding something to complain about," her mother said. Coretta was Elizabeth's youngest daughter. She and her husband, who had passed away some years ago, raised their four girls in a three-story row home in West Philadelphia.

Coretta stood up and walked to the edge of the porch. She grabbed hold of the iron railing and swung around as she had done as a child. "I'm not complaining. It's just that James is at work all day and he goes to school at night. I'm at home all day and I just feel like I should be doing something." Elizabeth narrowed her eyes and cocked her head to the side as she looked at Coretta. She didn't have to utter a word because Coretta knew the meaning of that look and immediately let go of the railing. "You're a new wife, Coretta," she said as she pulled her knitting needles from the basket that sat at her feet. With a little push, the wicker rocking chair began to sway back and forth. "There is no reason for you to be bored. Keeping house is not a small task. There is always some work to be done to keep a nice home."

"But that's just it, Mama. I've done all those things. The house is clean and with only the two of us there, it hardly ever gets messy. How long can it take to make one bed and run the vacuum? I just sit there all day reading or watching television. I don't think I can keep this up much longer."

Elizabeth chuckled. "Sounds to me like you need a hobby. Why don't you take up knitting or crocheting?"

"I don't need a hobby, mother. I need a life. I need something important to do with my life."

Elizabeth dropped her knitting into her lap. "And you think that being a homemaker is not important. Is that what you're telling me, Coretta?"

"No mother, it just isn't the life I want."

"So, what are you saying Coretta? Is it that you don't want to be married anymore? Do you want a divorce?"

Coretta sat down beside her mother. "No Mama. I just want something to do with my life. I want to go back to school, learn something I can do with my life."

"But I thought that you and James agreed that he would go to school first and after he has a degree and a job, then you can go back to school."

"I know, but I think that was a mistake. James is in school part-time. It may take five or six years before he has a degree. I can't wait that long."

"You'll feel different once the babies start coming." Elizabeth said with a knowing smile.

Coretta didn't answer. With so much time on her hands, she spent many hours thinking about her life and she had begun to think that every decision she'd made since graduating from high school had been a mistake. She wasn't even sure she wanted babies or even to be married.

> *"Therefore, shall a man leave his father and his mother, and shall cleave unto his wife: and they shall be one flesh." Genesis 2:24*

The words of that scripture sounded in Coretta's head like an alarm. She couldn't remember how many times she had heard this verse in sermons, prayers at home, and even as part of the grace, they said before meals. It was as if she and her sisters were programed to be married. She never even considered a life without marriage. Thinking back, she now wondered if James had truly been her choice or her parents. Of course, this was the example her parents lived before she and her sisters to see. Her parents had been married for thirty-five years and she couldn't remember a time when they weren't in complete sync.

"Maybe I'll get a job," she said.

"If you won't be at home, who will cook supper for your husband?"

"James isn't an invalid, Mom. He may have to learn to cook his own supper."

Elizabeth narrowed her eyes again but this time, the effect on Coretta was far different. Coretta turned and faced her mother. Their eyes locked for several seconds before Elizabeth's attention went back to her knitting. She sat with her reading glasses perched low on her plain, make-up free face. Her gray hair was cropped short and she wore a flowered housedress. The only sound was Elizabeth's plastic knitting needles clicking against one another. "Mom, where did you get that hideous dress?"

The question shocked Elizabeth and she lifted her head with pure bewilderment on her face. "I've got quite a few of these dresses, Coretta. I order them from my ladies catalogue. Why?"

As Coretta stood there in the shade of the trees that hung over the porch, the faint scent of honeysuckle floated in the air and she suddenly saw her Mother differently. Elizabeth Willis was exactly who she wanted to be but she wasn't who

Coretta wanted to be. It was as plain as if it were written across the sky and Coretta wondered why she had never realized that her well-meaning parents had gently manipulated their children into the lives that they wanted for them.

A sudden urge to strike out for her own independence seized her. "No reason. I just thought that they stopped making housedresses back in the 1960s." As soon as Coretta finished the sentence, she was sorry. "I'm sorry, Mom. I didn't mean to hurt your feelings."

Elizabeth smiled and went back to her knitting. She kept her head down as she spoke. "You think because you don't like my dress, that you've hurt my feelings? Let me tell you something, Coretta." Still she did not look up from her knitting. "I am comfortable with who I am. I have never had dreams of being any more than who I already am. I wanted to be a good Christian, a good wife and a good mother. I feel as if I have accomplished all that I ever dreamed and I'm good with that. It seems to me that instead of finding fault with me, you ought to be taking a more serious look at yourself."

The entire time she spoke, Coretta was looking at her mother. She realized that she had no desire to be her mother and her mother's words gave her permission to be whoever she desired to be. "I'm still sorry. I don't know what got into me to say something so mean spirited."

"Apology accepted," Elizabeth said.

Coretta left her mother's home and headed over to visit with June, the middle sister. June lived in Germantown, all the way on the other side of town. Before she even parked the car, she could hear June's high-pitched voice yelling at her oldest son. "Danny, get down from there. You're going to fall." The voices came from the back of the house and Coretta walked around the side of the house to the back yard. Danny was climbing a tree as if he hadn't heard his mother's warning. June was feeding her three-year-old twin girls who sat in a double high chair, while her four-month-old daughter wailed away in the pack-n-play. She never even heard Coretta and didn't look up until she saw Coretta lift Danny down from a low hanging branch. "Hi Coretta, what brings you over this afternoon?"

"I wanted to talk but I see now that it wasn't a good idea. You've got your hands full."

"Danny, if you go near that tree again, you're going to get a time-out!" she said. To Coretta, "Yeah! My hands are always full. I've got four children, Coretta. Now is as good a time as any."

"I see," Coretta said as she slumped down in one of the lawn chairs.

"So, what did you want to talk about?"

Coretta walked over and lifted baby Nicole out of the pack-n-play. She put Nicole on her shoulder and gently bounced as she rubbed the baby's back to sooth her. Nicole gurgled a little then stopped crying. "Are you happy, June?" she asked. "I mean, are you really happy with your life?"

"Wow," June said as she looked up at her sister. "Is this going to be one of your woe is me conversations; because if it is Coretta, I don't have time for this nonsense right now."

"June, I'm serious. I just don't know if I'm cut out for the whole wife and mother thing. I think I want to do something different with my life."

"Ok, so what's stopping you?"

"I really don't know what I want to do and I'm not sure how James will take it when I tell him I want to go to school."

"But I thought . . ."

"I know," Coretta cut her off. "I can't wait until he finishes. It could be years." She felt the gentle mummer of Nicole snoring against her shoulder. Out of the corner of her eye, she saw her nephew push his toy dump truck toward her. He had filled the back with wet soil.

"Beep, beep," said Danny. "You're standing on the highway Aunt Coretta."

Coretta stepped aside and Danny proceeded to dump his load of mud and stones into her purse that she had casually dropped before she retrieved him from the tree.

"Danny, no!" Both Coretta and June screamed but it was too late. At first Coretta was angry but her anger quickly faded.

"Oh, Coretta, I'm so sorry," June said. "Danny, that's it. You're in time-out." She grabbed him by the arm and led him to a child size chair by the back door. "You will sit here until nap time. Now, apologize to your aunt."

"Sorry, Aunt Coretta," he said sheepishly.

Coretta just nodded at Danny before she laid the sleeping Nicole back in the pack-n-play. "Well, I'm certain about one thing," Coretta said.

"Yeah, what's that?"

"There will be no children anytime soon." With that, the sisters began to laugh. It was an infectious laugh, as it had happened many times when they were children. The more June laughed, the more Coretta laughed. Eventually the twins began to laugh and Danny, sitting all alone in the corner began to laugh also.

When the giggles finally subsided, June said, "Go home Coretta and discuss this with your husband. There is nothing wrong with changing your mine. If you want to go to school, then go. James is a reasonable man. He'll understand."

"I know, I just didn't want to tell him until I was sure of exactly what I wanted to do and I still don't know." Coretta began to empty the contents of her purse to clean off the dirt.

"Where is your passion, Coretta?"

"What do you mean?"

"I mean, what drives you? I knew from the time I was fourteen that I wanted to be married and have children. I love children. If my children hadn't come so quickly after marriage, I would have probably wanted to be a teacher or a daycare provider. My passion is children, Coretta. You have to figure out what it is you love and then go from there."

Coretta stayed to help June get the children down for their nap before heading home. As she drove over the winding road of Lincoln Drive, all she could think about was what June said. What was her passion, she wondered? She thought about calling her older sister, Dawn, but quickly changed her mind. Dawn was also a mother and wife but her husband was a minister. When she wasn't at home with the children, she was working in the church. Her life was more than full and she would probably give her the same advice June had given.

It was near ten when James finally came home. Coretta waited up for him, which was unusual. "Hey Babe," he said as he came through the door.

"Hey."

"Why are you still awake?"

"I wanted to talk."

"All right," he said as he dropped his bag in a chair and headed for the kitchen. Coretta followed. "What is it, Coretta?" He put the plate of spaghetti Coretta had prepared for him into the microwave and turned it on. "Well, what's going on," he said impatiently. "I'm tired Coretta and I still have a lot of reading to do. What's on your mind?"

Suddenly, Coretta didn't want to have this conversation. She didn't feel this was the best time to approach James with her concerns. "Nothing," she said softly.

"Nothing," he repeated. He sat down and began to eat. With his mouth full, he said, "You waited up for me to tell me nothing? Come on Coretta. Let's talk."

Coretta poured James a glass of peach tea and sat down at the table with him. "I want to go to school," she said.

"School?" he questioned. "Are you serious?"

"Yes James," she said softly. As if she were in a hurry to get it all out, she said, "I want to learn something that I can do with my life and I don't want to have children right away."

James dropped his fork and looked at his young wife. At first, his face was serious and then a broad smile spread across his face. "That's great, Coretta."

"I thought you would be angry."

"Why in the world would I be angry?"

"Because we agreed that you would be the one to go to school first."

"Coretta, I love you. If going to school is going to make you happy, I would never object." He stood up and pulled Coretta from her chair. He wrapped his strong arms around her and she leaned into his embrace feeling secure and happy. "It will be hard financially, with both of us in school but we'll make it work."

At that moment, Coretta was reminded why she had fallen in love with James. Besides being the handsomest man she knew, he was kind, generous, and loved her immensely. "Thank you," she said as she went up on her toes to kiss his cheek.

"For what?" he said. "I didn't do anything."

"Thank you for just being you, James."

"All right," he said smiling as he sat down to finish his dinner. Coretta sat down at the table across from James. "So, I guess you'll be going for your nursing degree?"

His words hit Coretta like a slap across the face. "Nursing? What would make you think about nursing?"

James looked puzzled. "Remember when Dawn had her appendix removed? You were at the hospital every day, making sure she got proper care, reading to her, and doing whatever you could to make her comfortable." He finished the last of his dinner before he went on. "And when your mother had minor surgery, you were the same way. It's like, you just jump in whenever someone gets sick. I've always thought that you enjoyed taking care of people who were sick."

Coretta was flabbergasted. James was right. Whenever someone she loved was ill, she would do her best to help him or her through their illness. It made her feel needed. She couldn't believe that she had never even considered nursing. Was this really her passion, as June said? "Wow," she said now. "James, I think you know me better than I know myself."

James smiled. "Let's go up to bed, honey. I've got a ton of reading before I go to sleep." He took Coretta by the hand and they went up to bed. After they were both in bed, James read from an engineering book while Coretta took out her laptop to research nursing programs. "I hear that Jefferson has one of the best nursing programs in the city," James said.

"Then I guess I'll be a nursing student at Jefferson this fall."

"And I'll be the proudest husband in Philly."

BLIND JUDGEMENT

"You smell!"

"So do you."

"Yeah, but you smell so bad that even the rats don't want to get too close to you."

"Can't see no rats, but I *can* smell you," Griffin taunted the younger man. "How long you been without a bath?"

Walter didn't answer right away. The space between the two men seemed to stretch in the short silence. "Long as you," Walt finally said.

"You don't know how long I been without a bath," Griffin answered indignantly. "I didn't even know you before today and, in fact, I smelled you before I met you."

"Oh, that's real funny old man. Take a bow."

This time the silence was even longer and they seemed to grow even further apart. The only sound in the dark alley was that of the consistent drip of rainwater through an old storm drain. Griffin shifted his feeble body trying to find some semblance of comfort atop the mound of plastic trash bags. "Ain't never seen a rat," he whispered again.

"Huh?"

"I said, I ain't never seen a rat!"

"No foolin." Walt said in disbelief. "Well I seen plenty. Just how long you been callin this here alley home without seein a rat?"

"I'm not sure," the old man thought for a while. "I think maybe a year, give or take a month. I kind of lose track of time out here."

"You mean to tell me that you been down here a whole year and you ain't never seen a rat?"

"Nope."

"Wow! I can't hardly believe that Griff. Every time I open my eyes, the first thing I look for is rats. They bite, you know?"

"Never thought about it."

"Yeah, they bite and they eat most anything. I'm always on the lookout for the big nasty critters. If I went one day without seein a rat, I'd think I was dead and gone to heaven." Walt shivered at the thought. Not that he was afraid of rats; of course, he just didn't like the critters.

"It ain't that hard to believe. I'm blind."

"Blind?"

"Yeah, that's what I said. I'm blind."

Again, Walter was shocked. He propped himself on one elbow and leaned closer. "Griff, you mean you can't see anything?"

"Not a damn thing."

It was quiet again but this time the silence didn't seem to separate the two men. Walter didn't know what to say. He wanted to know if Griffin had always been blind or if he'd been the victim of some horrible accident but he wouldn't dare ask. He'd learned that people don't like other people that ask too many questions. So, he waited hoping that Griffin would offer something to assuage his curiosity but Griffin said no more.

Walter had lived on the streets of Philadelphia for more than two years and he had met many people. He met all types of people who found themselves living on the street, either purely by fate or by choice, but Walter had never met a blind man on the street before Griff. Finally, his curiosity got the best of him and he said, "How?"

"How, what?"

"How can you survive on the street being blind? These streets ain't no picnic for folk with two seeing eyes. I just don't understand how you survive."

"I survive same as you. I eat where and when I can and I sleep the same way."

"Oh," was all Walter said.

"How did you come to be on the street Walter?" Griffin asked.

"How do you think? Probably the same as everybody else out here, I lost my job. No work, no income, no home. That about covers it for everyone out here except the ones they let out of them mental hospitals."

"Not me," Griff said.

"What do you mean, not you?"

"I mean, I didn't have a job to lose. I just left."

"Why?"

"I left Georgia a few years back to come to live with my daughter. She married some high powered Philadelphia attorney named Allman. Everything was all right for a while. Then he decides he wants me out of their condo and in some home. They argued about it for a while and I just decided that I would die rather than see my little girl so unhappy so I just left."

"You left?"

"Yep. I just walked right out the door and I ain't looked back."

"So you think your little girl is happy not knowing where her daddy is or how he's doing?"

Griff was quiet for a moment. Of course, he had thought of the things Walt said many times but he figured his daughter would get over that grief in time. "She may have worried at first but it's been about a year now. I'm sure she's over it."

"That's too bad. I guess you miss her, huh?"

"I miss everything but I'd rather miss her out here where I'm not a burden to her and I'm not cooped up in some home where people thirty years younger than me want to tell me when to wake up, when to sleep or eat. No freedom, you know what I mean?"

"Yeah, I know exactly what you mean."

Quiet minutes passed and Walt finally heard the old man softly snoring. He crawled into the card board box that would serve as his bed for the night and went to sleep. Just before dawn, a chorus of whining cats in the alley jarred Walt awake. He lay there for a few minutes planning his day in the quiet of the early morning. It was early March and the worst of the winter was behind them but with March came rain, sometimes icy rain. Walter's shoes had a hole worn right through to the sole. Although he'd padded the soles, with newspapers and pieces of plastic nothing seemed to stop the dampness from seeping through. His chosen mission today was to find a pair of shoes. There was a mission over on Arch Street where the city gave away shoes, blankets and some clothes to the homeless but Walt preferred to find his shoes by trash picking or panhandling enough to pay for a pair of second hand shoes. He made it a practice to stay away from the missions. Those people at the missions were always trying to put you away. They would send you to a shelter or a hospital where the people would clean you up, feed you and then treat you as if you weren't just homeless but lazy, stupid or crazy. No, He'd stick to trash picking.

"Hey Griff, you awake?"

When Griff didn't answer, Walter knew that he'd already left the alley.

Two years of panhandling had taught Walter that people were more willing to give if they thought that you were homeless through no fault of your own, so he had taken to wearing a sign that read, "DEAF MUTE." Wearing that sign was the biggest lie Walter had ever told but it always brought him more money than just begging alone.

With his sign hanging from his shoulders, Walt took his plastic shopping bag and headed for the street. By noon, Walt had enough money to get a hamburger and a two dollar pair shoes from the second hand shop on Market Street. Even thought it was a cold and rainy day the manager of the fast food restaurant where Walt bought his hamburger said that he couldn't eat inside the store. "I'm sorry, but you'll have to leave the store," said a pimple and freckled face young man that Walt assumed was the manager. "You're scaring away the customers and you stink. Just take your order and go outside."

"You didn't give me this hamburger, you know. I paid for it same as everyone else. That makes me a customer too."

The young man flagged Walter and went back inside the store. This wasn't the first time Walter had been asked to leave a restaurant and Walt knew that there was no sense arguing with managers. The manager would just call the police and he'd be asked to leave anyway. Walt pretended to kick the door but in the end, he just walked away. He decided to eat his hamburger in the little park across the street. He found an empty bench where he sat and ate his burger slowly, savoring the familiar taste. It wasn't much but it was certainly enough to take the edge off of his hunger for a while.

Now that he had warm dry shoes on his feet and a little something in his belly, Walt decided that it was time to scrounge enough money for dinner and start looking for a place to sleep. He made his way toward the park exit. He noticed about five teenage boys on the other side of the park. They bounced a basketball and laughed playfully along until they came upon a homeless man. One of them, a tall blonde kid said something to the man and his friends roared with laughter. Walter couldn't hear what the boy said but he could tell from the sneering faces of his friends that the words were probably not kind. Then the boy threw his basketball at the man. The man stumbled awkwardly toward his tormentors only to be struck a second time with the basketball. He yelled for help as the other boys joined their friend in an evil game of abuse, throwing bottles and stones at the helpless old man. The man grabbed hold of his cart and tried to move away from his abusers.

Lousy kids, Walt thought as his eyes scanned the park for a police officer.

"Help! Help!" The raspy voice was hardly able to pitch as high as a scream but it brought Walt's attention back to the scene. It was Griff.

Walter ran as fast as he could toward the group. "Leave him alone!" Walt shouted. One of the boys pushed Griffin's cart away from him and Griff fell, the side of his face slapping against the cement walkway. Walt swung at the group of boys with his shopping bag as his voice added to Griff's hoarse, barely audible screams for help. He was pushed down to the ground and kicked in his side until he could move no more. He and Griff lay only a few feet apart. No help came but the boys soon tired of their evil game. They walked away still laughing and playing as if they were proud of their wickedness. Griffin still screamed, although his cry was hardly more than a whisper. "It's alright Griff. It's me, Walter. Everything is alright buddy."

"Are they gone?"

"Yeah, they're gone. Think you can stand?" Walt asked as he heaved himself off of the ground. With Walter's help, Griff scrambled to his feet. Blood oozed from a gash at the side of his head, slightly below his temple. "Looks like you hit your head pretty hard. I think we should get you to a hospital."

"No!" Griff protested and tried to pull away from Walt's grip on his arm. "No hospitals."

"That gash on your head looks serious. You could need stitches or something."

"I don't care. I won't go to a hospital. You know as well as me that if I go to a hospital, I'll be in a home by suppertime. No hospital and no home, I won't go."

"Alright, alright, but we've got to do something to stop the bleeding. Walt rummaged through Griff's belongings until he found an old shirt. He tore it into rags and wrapped it securely around Griff's head. The rain had become steadier now and Walt knew that he should at least get Griffin to some place dry. They made their way east toward the waterfront. People rushed past them. Businessmen and women, students, and office workers and delivery workers all rushed pass them keeping pace with the urgency of their individual lives. Two homeless men in tattered and soiled clothes, one obviously hurt and the other struggling to carry his meager belongings, while supporting his injured friend. No one seemed to notice. In a city bustling with activity, they were invisible to society.

After they had walked about fifteen minutes or so, they came upon an abandoned office building on Second Street. Although they couldn't get into the building, they could get into the vestibule. Walt made Griff as comfortable as he could. He knew that he would have to leave to find some food for dinner and he worried about leaving Griff alone with his head still bleeding. Ignoring his fears and taking some comfort in the fact that the vestibule was at least dry, he promised to get back as soon as he could and he left Griff alone.

He returned two hours later with biscuits and fried chicken that he'd scavenged from a KFC dumpster. "Hey Griff, wake up man."

Griffin sat up sluggishly and opened his eyes. For the first-time Walt looked into the blank stare of blind eyes and he shivered as if a cold wind had blown straight through his body. The makeshift bandage that he used to wrap Griffin's head was soaked through with blood. "Hey Griff," he said again. "We've got to get some help for your head. You're bleeding again." Griffin didn't answer. He'd lost a lot of blood and Walter was afraid for his new friend. "Griff, maybe we should go into the shelter just for the night, ah?"

"No!"

"Why? You can't stay here man. Look how you're bleeding. This is serious man."

"I told you, no hospital."

"Why? Just tell me why?"

"Too many coons in the shelter."

"What?" Walt could hardly believe his ears. Sure, he'd only know this man for a couple of days but he never figured him for a racist.

"You heard me, too many coons. My Daddy told me that there is two kinds of people to stay clear of, whorin women and coons."

Walt wanted to laugh but instead he said, "Griff, have you ever known a coon?"

"No, but I knew a whorin woman once. Married her and she kept right on whorin with my kid in her belly and my ring on her finger. Now I figure, if my Daddy was right about her, he is probably right about the coons too." Walter couldn't believe what he was hearing. "You ever seen a coon, Walt?"

"Yeah, plenty, but my Daddy didn't call them coons."

"What did he call them?"

"People, Griff, just people." He filled Griffin's hands with chicken and biscuits and Griffin ate hungrily. "Guess you were pretty hungry, buddy?"

"Guess so. Why do you keep calling me buddy?"

"It's just an expression Griff. It means friend."

"Does that mean that I'm your friend?"

"Guess so."

Walt didn't sleep much that night. He worried that Griffin was losing too much blood. In the morning when Griff wouldn't wake up, Walt panicked. He remembered the name of Griffin's daughter. Griff had said that she married an attorney named Allman.

Leaving Griff alone in the vestibule again, Walt walked several blocks until he found a public telephone booth where the phone books had not been ripped from the walls. He went down the list of Allmans, making several collect calls and giving his name as Griffin. Finally, someone accepted the call and asked that he hold. He silently prayed as he waited. Then a soft voice came over the line, "Dad? I've been worried sick. Where are you?"

"Ah, my name is Walter, Ma'am. I know where your father is and he's been hurt."

"Where is he?"

Walter relayed the events of the past day to Griff's daughter and told her where she could find her father. Then he went back to the vestibule to wait. Three hours later Griffin had gotten stitches for his head wound; a blood transfusion for the loss of blood and was resting comfortably. Walter sat in the kitchen of a high-rise apartment building overlooking West River Drive and the Art Museum. He ate the first full meal he'd consumed in over a year.

"Mr. Walter, I can't tell you how grateful I am for all you've done for my father," Barbara Allman said. Griffin smiled between bites and Walt could tell that no matter what he'd said about freedom, he was happy to be at home.

"Mr. Walt," Mrs. Allman said. "I have to tell you that meeting you was rather a surprise for me. You are the first black friend my father as ever had."

Griffin dropped his fork and it made a loud clang as it hit the glass table. The shock that spread across his face was priceless, Walt thought. "I guess now you can say that even though you've never seen a coon, you are blessed to have a black man for a friend."

"I'm sorry. I didn't know," Griff said.

"It's alright buddy. I know you didn't know." Griff's face still held the look of shock. "It's alright buddy really," Walt said, "You see, out there on the street you are as black as I am to the world. We're both like pariahs in a pond of swans when we're on the street."

After taking a shower and a shave, Walt was given clean pajamas, a robe and slippers. Mrs. Allman said he could stay in the guest room. Walter didn't know just how far the Allman's gratitude would extend but he was grateful for just the night.

LOVE LETTERS

Richard Sheridan was once a robust and handsome man, great in stature and personality. His congenial character won him many friends and ladies fancy. Now at seventy-five his tall frame was hunched with age. His hearing had started to diminish some ten years earlier and was now almost completely gone. His body was weak and riddled with the common ailments of the aged.

Rick, as he was called in his younger years, had just loss his wife of forty years and was having a very difficult time moving past his grief. He sits in a wheel chair placed in front of a large picture window of the solarium in the Alden Elder Care Center, which has been Rick's home for more than a year now. His day nurse, Miss Jean, comes in to check his vitals as she does every day. Rick offers no resistance and places his left arm in Miss Jean's capable hands. When she is finished marking his chart she turns to get a better look at her patient. "Mr. Sheridan, your blood pressure is a little high today. What's going on with you? Is something bothering you, Mr. Sheridan?"

Rick doesn't answer and Miss Jean is not really expecting an answer anyway. He doesn't want to tell her that he is upset because today is the first day that he hasn't been able to picture his wife Lola. Even when he couldn't remember where he was or even his own name, he could still picture Lola. Her face, soft and smooth with big brown eyes was always smiling in the gaze of his mind's eye, but not today. Today he could see nothing. He just couldn't remember what she looked like.

It was early May and as Rick looked out of the window over the manicured lawns of the nursing home, he could see the lush green grass, and rose bushes that decorated the landscape. The flowers had not yet opened their delicate petals to full bloom. An odd feeling came over him. He knew that the rose held some special significance to him but he just couldn't remember what. He spent the day sitting in his wheel chair sulking in his private dilemma until he was finally helped to bed.

At his comfortable home in East Mt. Airy, Rick and Lola's only daughter, Denise was struggling with her own grief.

She and her mother were closer than the average mother and daughter. Even though she was seventy at the time of her passing, she had been blessed with a youthful spirit. Denise never saw her mother as old. She was beautiful, stylish, and still vivacious. Lola had refused to accept the limitation that society placed on the elderly. She was her own woman right up until her last breath. Because Lola's death was sudden and completely unexpected, it hit Denise like a sledge hammer.

Though she knew that her father was also suffering, Denise needed time to deal with her own grief before she could even hope to comfort her father. Now she was faced with the task of cleaning out her parent's home to make it ready for sale. Large crates were scattered about the house in almost every room. She decided early that the furniture would be sold as part of the estate but the walls must be cleared of all pictures, some of which had hung on those walls most of her life. She needed to empty every drawer, cupboard, and closet in the house. She had taken to the task like a robot, moving quickly with little thought, and almost no emotion. It was the only way she could get it all done. Now in the master bedroom Denise began to pack her mother's clothes and toiletries. As she picked up a small bottle of Red Door , her mother's favorite fragrance, she felt her resolve begin to crack and fall away like the pieces of a shattered mirror. She sank down onto the bed, tears flowing freely as she gave into her grief. How could they go on without her, she wondered even as she knew that they would go on without Lola. After all, Denise knew that death was an integral part of life. There was an end to everything and life was no exception.

She no longer tried to stifle her grief but let her tears flow praying that time would heal her wounds just a little sooner. Denise didn't know how long she had been crying but when she stopped, she felt as if she had managed to crawl from beneath a huge burden. She went to the bathroom and washed her face. She stood, straightening her back, pushing her shoulders back and setting her mind to finishing the task at hand.

Once the toiletries had been packed away, she began to clear the night tables. Her father's night table was nearly empty and very much what she expected. She found a few Ellery Queen Mystery Magazines, a recent issue of Jet Magazine and an old copy of The Heart of Darkness. The manicure kit that she'd given him for his birthday when she was just a kid was still neatly placed in its leather case as if it had never been used.

Her mother's bedside table was quite different. It was more than a little cluttered. It was filled with old greeting cards, personal medications, small photo brag books and a host of other mementoes. In the bottom drawer, Denise found some old letters. They were tied neatly together with an old satin ribbon. Denise got the strangest feeling when she picked up the bundle of letters. She felt as if she were entering a place where she didn't belong. Spurred on by pure curiosity Denise took the first letter from its crumbling envelope and began to read:

> *July 24, 1960. My Dearest Lola:*
> *It has rained for four days straight and I*
> *feel as if I will never see the sun again or*
> *feel the warmth of its rays touch my face.*
> *Seeing you, is the only thing I look*
> *forward to and I am counting the minutes*
> *until I can hold you in my arms again and*
> *kiss your sweet lips.*
> > *The thought of you is all that*
> *keeps me going. Both day and night, I*
> *reminisce about our last time together as I*

pray that we will be together again very
soon.

> *Please do not change, my*
> *sweet, and do not give up on me. I promise*
> *to come back to you as soon as I am able.*
> *Yours Only, Panda*

"Panda!" Denise said aloud. "Who the hell is Panda?" She quickly removed the second letter and began to read. All of the letters expressed the love and devotion of Panda. Some of them were just poems or love sonnets. She checked the outside of the envelopes again and they were all addressed to her mother with no return address. At first she assumed that the letters must be from her father but the more she read the more suspicious she became. By the time Denise opened the tenth letter, she was convinced that the letters were definitely not written by her father. She had a hard time believing that her father would ever call himself Panda.

What kind of name was Panda anyway? She didn't remember ever hearing about someone named Panda. She certainly didn't remember her parents ever being apart so that they would need to communicate through letters. Her parents hadn't even met until after her father had served in the military.

Denise took the bundle of letters and tied them together again with that same fragile piece of ribbon and stuffed them into her bag to take home with her. That night after Denise had put her own children to bed and her husband was fast asleep, she resumed reading the letters. There were twenty-four letters of love. When at last she read the final letter, she was convinced that her mother had had an affair with someone named Panda. Her emotions spun in all directions. She at first was outraged. How could Lola have done such an awful thing? However, as quickly as the thought came to her it was replaced with doubt.

No, she thought. There must be another explanation. Lola would never cheat on her father, but who was Panda? Did her father even know Panda?

The next day Denise told her husband Martin about the letters. "What do you think I should do, Martin?"

Martin took a long sip from his coffee mug and was thoughtful for a moment. Denise waited impatiently. Finally, he said, "Nothing! Lola has passed on, let her secret pass too."

"Martin," Denise was agitated. "We don't even know that this is a secret. Just because I didn't know about it doesn't make it a secret. Maybe Panda isn't a man at all. What if Panda is a woman?"

Martin didn't answer right away. He finished his breakfast, grabbed his jacket and briefcase, and headed for the door.

"Martin," Denise said again.

"Look honey, you asked me for my opinion and I gave it to you. I think that you should let this go. Forget you ever heard of Panda." With that, he was out of the door.

Despite Martin's advice, Panda was all Denise could think about, even at work she was unable to concentrate. She thought even if her mother had an affair back in 1960, that was over forty years ago. What could it matter now? Her parent's marriage had obviously survived the affair and her father could hardly feel betrayed after so many years. Besides there wasn't much he cared about these days anyway. Denise made up her mind that she would ask her father if he knew anyone named Panda. Even if Rick knew Panda, he might not remember him or her.

That evening Denise went to visit with her father right after work. By the time she arrived, it was near six in the evening and the sun had just begun to set. She found Rick sitting in his wheel chair facing the window in the solarium as usual.

"Hey Dad," she said as she bent to kiss his cheek. "It's getting dark outside Dad. Why are you facing the window? Would you like me to turn you around so you can watch television?"

"Na," he said rather gruffly. "There isn't anything on that tube worth watching."

Denise knew right away that something was wrong. "What's wrong? Did something happen? Are you not feeling well?"

"Oh, stop fussing, I'm fine."

"You don't look fine. Don't lie to me Dad. I can tell when something is bothering you."

"I can't picture her."

"Who?"

"Your mother. I can't see her face anymore. I've been sitting here for two days trying to remember what she looked like and I can't picture her. It just won't come to me. I can't remember what she looked like."

Denise watched her father's agony. "It will come back to you Dad. Just give it time."

"You don't understand baby. I need to see her face. It's the only thing that makes me happy."

Denise stared at her father both marveling at the love he still felt for Lola and overwhelmed with the sadness of knowing that he will never really see her again. She reached into her bag and took out her wallet. She handed Rick a small photo that had been taken only a couple of years ago. Rick took one look at the photo and then pressed it to his chest as his glazed eyes welled with new tears.

"Thank you," he said softly.

"Dad, we've got lots of photos. You'll always be able to look at Mom's face in photos."

"I know that but I just wanted to remember her. I wanted to close my eyes and see her just the way she was when she was my Poo Bear and I was her Panda Bear."

"Panda?" Denise said. "Mom called you Panda?"

"Yeah, but that was years ago, long before you were born."

Denise burst into laughter, which quickly turned into sobs as she realized how ridiculous she was to think that her mother would ever have an affair. She reached into her bag again and brought out the letters. "Dad, you mean to tell me that you wrote all of these letters?" she asked as she handed the bundle to him.

Rick smiled as he took the bundle of letters from his daughter. "I can't believe your mother saved all of these letters." His joy was written all over his face and he continued to smile.

"Dad, I was angry when I found those letters. I thought Mom had an affair with someone named Panda."

Rick threw his head back as he laughed hysterically. It was a hardy laugh, deep and strong the way he used to laugh before illness and age had weakened his body. Suddenly there was no trace of the weak shaky voice, which Denise had become accustomed to lately. He leaned forward and took his daughter's hand, pulling her to him. He kissed her cheek and gave her a strong embrace. "You brought me happiness today, Nicey. Thank you."

"Oh Dad, you know that you're welcome. It's good to see you happy for a change."

They sat quietly for a few moments, each consumed with their own memories of Lola. "Dad, you know the reason you're here at Alden was because you needed round the clock care and Mom just couldn't do it."

"I know, honey."

"She put you here because she wanted you to be close so she could visit whenever she wanted. She didn't want to have to travel too far."

"Yes, I know that too."

"Well, what would you say about moving in with Martin and me and the kids. You know that Martin and I can afford a full time nurse and God knows we have the room."

"I'd say when do we leave?"

They both laughed again.

"It will take me a couple of days to make things ready for you. We'll need to get your room ready and hire a nurse."

"It's alright Denise. I'm not going anywhere. Whenever you and Martin are ready, I'll be waiting."

"Oh Dad, I can't tell you how good it is to see you smile again."

She kissed him again on the cheek and prepared to leave. She suddenly stopped and turned to face her father again. "Hey, why were you and Mom writing letters in the first place?"

"It was kind of a game, something your mother started because she thought it would keep life in our marriage. We were young and stupid, crazy in love and she decided that we would take on nick-names and pretend that we were in different cities. We'd send a letter at least once a month. So you see, it really was as if she was having an affair with this guy named Panda. I pretended to be in the military stationed in Viet Nam and she was my sweetheart waiting for me here in the states. Sometimes we would even plan a rendezvous and take a room in one of the expensive hotels down town. We kept the game going for two years but once you were born there wasn't much time for playing games anymore."

"Why did the letters smell like roses?"

Rick had forgotten about the roses until the second Denise mentioned them. "I use to put rose petals in the envelopes before I mailed the letters." He smiled to himself realizing that another piece to his mystery was solved. The smile became even broader when he remembered how excited Lola was every time she got a letter from Panda.

"You know your mother was right. That silly little game of hers did keep our marriage fresh and new for a long time. It might not be a bad idea if you and Martin started writing letters."

"Maybe not letter writing but I'd be a fool if I didn't look at you and Mom's marriage as a shining example of how to make a marriage work."

HIND SIGHT

Thursday night was girl's night out and Leah Jones and her friends had fallen in love with a little restaurant named Anton's, which was inconspicuously tucked into a tiny alcove in Old City Philadelphia. The food was good and the service was even better. The three friends would meet every Thursday to laugh and talk away the pressures of the work-week. Thursday night was quickly becoming Leah's favorite night of the week, but that was soon to change.

It was one of those Thursdays that Leah had been looking forward to since the beginning of the week. Work had been especially chaotic, and Leah was looking forward to winding down and getting a head start on a relaxing weekend. This particular Thursday, a young waiter came to take the girls orders and Leah noticed that he was especially good looking, though he did look a bit young. He looked like a kid bussing tables as his after school job. Leah would later learn that he was neither a kid nor a waiter. His height was average, probably not even six feet, but his skin was a smooth chocolate brown. He didn't seem to be the athletic type but he was certainly lean and it was probably natural. There were no bulging biceps or dancing pecks. Leah guessed that if he did any exercise at all, he was probably a jogger.

"May I take your order?" His voice was deeper than Leah expected but very soft.

Later, when he returned with their orders, Leah couldn't help stealing another glance at the handsome young waiter, but when she looked up at him, she caught him also looking at her. Call it a spark or a connection; Leah didn't know what it was, but she knew something happened when their eyes met. He had big brown eyes with lids that looked as if they were about to close at any second. Some might even call his eyes "bedroom eyes." What Leah couldn't help noticing was the way he looked at her with those eyes. They seemed to penetrate through every layer of her essence, right down to her soul, which made Leah little uncomfortable. She shifted in her seat and pretended disinterest. He was fine but because Leah thought that he was too young, she silently acknowledged that fact to herself and quickly averted her attention.

"Didn't you see that waiter checking you out?" asked Felicia.

"No, I wasn't paying attention," Leah lied.

"Now you're lying," Joyce said. "I saw the two of you making eyes at each other. You saw him Leah and he saw you." They all laughed.

"Please! That boy is almost young enough to be my son. You're both being ridiculous."

"He might be young enough to be your son but he isn't your son," Joyce said.

"Yeah, he sure didn't look at you like a son looks at his Mama," Felicia put in.

"Alright, alright," Leah said. "You've both made your point now let's just drop it, alright." Leah quickly changed the subject and the three started talking about work and the cruise they were planning for later that year. What Leah's friends didn't know was that after she had paid for the evening's meal, the young waiter had written his phone number on the back of her credit card receipt. For two whole days, Leah carried that receipt around in her handbag, pulling it out several times a day just to stare at it. She debated with herself the pros and cons of calling him. Hell, she had just untangled herself from a five-year possessive and abusive relationship and really couldn't see herself in another relationship so soon. She didn't even know his name. All of her trepidations aside, on the third day Leah made the call.

"Hello, my name is Leah. I think you were our waiter at Anton's Thursday night." Leah felt like a fool. Suppose the man that answered the phone was the waiter's father or brother.

"Oh yeah, you were the short one with the curly hair, right?"

Leah relaxed. "Yes."

"What took you so long to call?"

"You didn't write your name on the receipt."

"Oh, that was stupid of me." He laughed. "I'm Anton."

"Anton? You mean you own the restaurant."

"Yes. I was just waiting tables because we were short-handed that Thursday."

Again, Leah felt like a fool. "Well, I must say you look too young to own such a popular and well established restaurant."

"Yeah, I've been told that before."

"How long have you owned the restaurant?"

"It's been about six years now."

"How old are you, if you don't mind me asking?" Leah knew her question was inappropriate, but she felt that she just had to ask.

"Why? Does it really matter?"

"Well, I think it might. I don't want to rob the cradle, as they say. I'd have second thoughts about dating someone too much younger than me."

"I haven't asked you for a date."

Leah didn't answer. She was now thoroughly humiliated and maybe a little angry. She started to hang up but when Anton snickered, she thought about it and knew that she may have deserved his biting remark. "Touché!" she whispered.

That was how their relationship began. It would end far differently. Anton was a charmer. He exuded a quiet, unpretentious charm that drew people closer to him. Leah wasn't even aware of when he actually captured her heart. Either by nature or by design, he had mastered the rules of seduction with the ease and competence of a playboy. Leah was hardly aware that she was being pursued, let alone taken captive. But, that was exactly what happened. Anton captured her heart, soul, and body.

They shared many late night telephone conversations, which quickly moved from twice a week to almost every night. Anton's smooth velvet voice was the first she heard in the morning and the last she heard before she fell asleep, which fueled her dreams. She dined at the restaurant a couple of nights a week and they began to spend almost every weekend together.

Their love-making was feverish. Though Leah had never considered herself a prude or matronly in any way, what Anton brought to her bed still made her blush to even think about it. Anton made her feel like a teenager and she couldn't get enough of him. As far as she could tell, he felt the same. No matter how many times she told herself that she didn't want to be in a committed relationship, it didn't change how she felt about Anton. She was falling head over heels in love with him and she couldn't stop.

There was nothing especially different or surprising about the building of their relationship except that it happened so quickly. Within a couple of months, Anton had a key to Leah's apartment and she was never surprised to come home and find him lounging on her sofa watching television. The two had been a couple for about four months when Leah decided that she should introduce Anton to her friends and family. She arranged a dinner party and invited her best friends, her sister, brother, and her parents. For a week, she drove herself crazy trying to see to every possible detail. She wanted a perfect evening. Anton agreed to do all of the cooking at the restaurant and have the food brought over to her apartment.

Leah was grateful that Felicia, Joyce and their dates arrived first. At least they'd already met Anton. Her parents were the second arrivals. Leah's father, a six foot three retired police detective, was quiet and a little standoffish. He never said much but he saw everything. "Hi Dad," she said as she went up on her toes to kiss his bearded cheek.

"Hey baby," was all he said. He took off his coat and hung it over his arm.

"I'll take that," Anton said. Mr. Jones hardly looked at Anton as he handed over his overcoat.

"Hey Mom," Leah said.

"Hi Baby," Mrs. Jones said. "The apartment looks great."

"Thank you." Leah took both her parent's hands and pulled them toward Anton. "There's someone I'd like for you two to meet. Mom, Dad, this is my friend Anton."

"You mean your boyfriend?" her Dad asked.

Anton smiled and in his usual self-assured manner, he stepped in to save Leah from an awkward moment. He pushed his hand forward to shake Mr. Jones hand. "Yes sir, Leah and I are a couple." Noticeable seconds passed as Anton stood with his hand extended for the customary 'I am a man too' shake. The moment lasted just long enough to make the point that Mr. Jones had no intention of accepting Anton as friend or family but if he didn't shake the young man's hand he would be the one to appear unreasonable and rude. He took his hand firmly as if to remind the young man that he was the stronger of the two despite his advancing years. Anton flashed the same handsome smile that made women blush and eventually brought a smile to Mr. Jones lips.

Mrs. Jones surprise was written all over her face but she did her best to conceal her true feelings as she extended her hand to the young man. "I'm very happy to meet you Anton. Leah tells me that you are a restaurant owner."

"Yes ma'am."

"That's nice."

As soon as Leah was alone for a moment, she was scooped up by her mother and rushed to the kitchen. "Leah, are you out of your mind? That is a boy in there."

"He's not a boy, Mom. He's a grown man."

"You will be thirty-five your next birthday and that young man can't be more than twenty-one or two."

"He's an adult, Mom," Leah said as she busied herself around the kitchen. "We are both adults. Please don't try to make me feel bad about the best thing that's happened in my life in years."

"I'm not trying to make you feel bad. I just want you to think about what you're doing."

The rest of the evening was for the most part uneventful. She introduced Anton to her sister Nicki and her brother Rasheem and both seemed as unconcerned about meeting Anton as they did about anything else that didn't directly affect them. Overall, the evening went well and Leah was thankful that it was over.

Leah and Anton's relationship continued along the same as it had begun for nearly a year. They took their vacations together, spent every holiday together with one or the other of their families. Anton's family consisted of his mother and grandmother, both of whom resided in South Carolina. His family happily accepted Leah as part of the family and she liked both women instantly.

Leah was a happy woman. Her career as a real estate agent was progressing smoothly and Anton's restaurant was featured in Philadelphia Magazine, which increased his patronage considerably. He was now considering opening a second Anton's in the western suburbs of Philadelphia.

Though the issue of age never came up again in making arrangements for their cruise to Jamaica, Leah learned that Anton was twenty-eight. This new knowledge made no difference in their relationship but still, something between them began to change.

It started around Thanksgiving. They were having dinner at her parent's house. Even though Anton was a chef and the owner of his own restaurant, Leah had assumed that he would be happy for a day when he wasn't expected to cook and spend the afternoon in the living room with her father and brother watching football. She could not have imagined that he would spend the entire day in the kitchen trying to school her mother on cooking the same thanksgiving dinner she had been cooking for over thirty-five years. At first, he was just annoying, but soon Leah thought her mother would explode if she didn't get Anton out of that kitchen. She suggested that they take a walk to a convenience store. Once out of the house she said, "You know Anton, my mother has been cooking thanksgiving dinner for our family for a very long time. She really doesn't need your help." Leah didn't want an argument to ensue so she spoke in what she thought was an even tone but it didn't matter. Anton flew into a rage anyway.

"That woman doesn't know the first thing about cooking. That's what's wrong with black people. They never want to learn anything new. I was just trying to show her something new."

Leah was stunned. "Now, hold on Anton! That's my mother you're talking about and how dare you smear black people like you're not black yourself."

"I don't give a damn. She can't cook, Leah," he screamed.

"She's not a chef, Anton, but she *is* my mother and I won't have you talk like that about her or disrespect her in her own home." Leah turned and walked away. She only took a few steps away before Anton ran to catch up to her. He grabbed her by the shoulders and swung her around to face him. He looked like a boy who had just lost his favorite toy. Tears clouded his eyes. "I'm sorry Leah. Please say you forgive me?"

Leah just looked at the tears that were now streaming down his face. He wiped at his face with the back of his hand and sniffed. "I'm not sure I'm ready to forgive you Anton. This is all so stupid. I can't believe you would be so worked up about something so trivial. What's happening with you?"

"You're right. It was really stupid of me." The tears vanished just as quickly as they had appeared. "It's just that I love cooking. It's what I do." He paused as if he were searching for the word that could make this all better. He sniffed again and again.

Leah began to walk back toward the house and Anton walked a few paces behind her. All she could think about was how he just flew into such a rage over some tiny little disagreement. They'd been together more than a year and she had never witnessed anything like this before. Suddenly she stopped walking and turned to face him. She wanted to tell him that she would forgive him and that she wanted more than anything, to forget that this entire incident had ever happened, but when she looked in his face, she was speechless. There he stood, his breath making clouds of smoke in the cold air, his eyes wide and red as fire and a tiny stream of blood leaked from his nostrils and he sniffed.

"You're bleeding," she said. "Your nose is bleeding." She handed him a tissue from her pocket. "Clean yourself up. We can't go back into my parent's house with you looking like that. What the hell is wrong with you?"

"I'm sorry Leah. I really didn't mean to blow up like that."

"Yeah," was all Leah said.

Leah's family knew that she and Anton had an argument. For the rest of the day everyone spoke in whispered tones as if they thought their voices were enough to send Anton into another rage. Mrs. Jones was especially unhappy. Before that day Anton's age was the only thing she saw as a possible problem, now she just didn't like him. All through dinner, she just kept looking from Anton to Leah with a strange look on her face. Leah knew that her mother was just itching to tell her how she felt about Anton but Leah had no intention of giving her mother a chance to lampoon her.

By the first of the New Year, it seemed that things had gotten back to normal. Over the Christmas holiday, Anton more than made up for his one night of questionable behavior. At Christmas he lavished Leah and her family with expensive gifts and on New Year' Eve he invited them all to dinner at his restaurant. He took that opportunity to apologize to the entire family in his usual charming manner. It seemed that they were all accepting of his heartfelt apology.

However, by April, Anton seemed to be spiraling out of control again. His behavior raged from frenzied to near catatonic. There were times when Leah didn't see him for days. He wouldn't show up at the restaurant or her apartment or answer the telephone. There were other times when he seemed on top of the world. He would run around in a frenzy. Leah may have had her suspicions but she pushed them to the back of her mind, not wanting to admit even to herself that there was a serious problem. It would be her friend Felicia who would actually voice what everyone in their circle thought.

It was girl's night out and the restaurant was extremely busy. Anton was full of energy as he moved back and forth from the kitchen to the dining room. He shouted orders to his staff and actually loudly ridiculed a young waitress. "What the hell are you doing?" he screamed. The young woman had not taken an order properly and the customer complained. "Can't you take a simple order? Are you stupid?"

The entire restaurant stopped and watched as the young waitress took her apron off and threw it at Anton. Tears streamed down her face as she ran from the dining room. Leah was embarrassed. "Umm," Felicia said. "Anton's acting like a coke head."

Leah knew that what Felicia said was right. Anton was acting as if he was high on something but Leah refused to believe that Anton could be using drugs. She thought about confronting him on the issue but she didn't want to deal with the consequences of it being true. She loved Anton more than she ever thought possible and she couldn't help being afraid of what this would mean to their relationship. She didn't call Anton that evening after the restaurant closed. When he called her, she feigned a headache and hung up quickly. Then Felicia called.

"Hello, Leah."

"Yeah."

"I'm calling to apologize."

"For what?"

"I'm sorry I called Anton a coke head. I don't know what I was thinking."

"Yes you did and you might be right so don't apologize to me." There was silence for a couple of seconds. "What am I going to do, Felicia?"

"You should talk with him. Maybe it isn't drugs."

"No. I think you were right the first time. This wasn't the first time I've seen him act that way." Again, there was silence.

"Look girl! Confront him and tell him that he needs to get some help or it's over."

"Oh come on Felicia! I can't give him an ultimatum like that. I love him and I am really afraid of losing him. I can't just abandon him. He'll need me to survive this and I love him too much to just walk away."

"Leah I'm telling you this because I love you. You are my best friend and I don't want that to change but if you don't get out of this now, he'll bring you down with him."

Leah was thoughtful for a moment. "You're wrong Felicia. I won't let that happen."

"If you're thinking that he cares about you more than the drug, I can tell you that you are absolutely wrong. I've seen this before. Coke will take over his life. Oh yeah, he may seem to be functioning as usual, but that is because this is only the beginning. If he's addicted, and I think he is, coke is the only thing he cares about right now."

"Felicia, I really hope that you're wrong. Hell, we're doing a lot of assuming. We don't even know that he's taking the drug, let alone an addict."

"Alright, then confront him."

There was silence on the line as Leah tried to wrap her mind around this entire situation. "Felicia, I really hope that you're wrong," she said again.

"Just confront him Leah. At least then you'll know what you're dealing with."

"I will, I promise I'll confront him soon."

The next day Leah called out from work. All she wanted to do was stay in bed. Just the thought of Anton being addicted to drugs was wearing her out and she just wanted to rest. It was about eleven in the morning when she heard Anton's key open the door.

He bounced into the bedroom, "Hey Leah, where've you been? I've been calling you all night and this morning."

"We have to talk Anton."

"Alright," he said pulling off his jacket and sitting on the edge of her bed.

"You've been acting kind of strange lately and I just want to know what's going on with you."

"What's going on with me? Nothing!

"This is serious Anton. Please be honest with me."

"Be honest about what?"

The look in his glassy eyes told Leah that the rage was coming. Leah watched as he stood up quickly. Both hands hung at his side but were clenched into tight fists. "I love you Anton. I only want what's best for both of us. I know that there is something terribly wrong. Just talk to me."

In one quick movement that made Leah jump, he turned around with both his hands raised and his arms stretched outward. He stomped his feet, all the while yelling, "I don't know what the hell you're talking about Leah!" Pictures frames fell from the wall and shattered glass sprung up from the floor. Leah jumped and up moved to the other side of her bed.

"This!" she screamed. "This is what I'm talking about. Why are you so angry? One day you're curled up on the sofa not far from a coma and the next you're ranting and raving like a mad man. I want to know why. I want to know what is happening."

In two long strides, he was right in front of her and for the first time Leah was actually afraid of Anton. At that moment, he looked as if he hated her and she shrank away from him to the far corner of the room. Frightened into silence, Leah just stood there cringing as Anton lifted his fist as if to strike her. The punch landed on the wall making a sizable hole and Leah screamed.

"Leave!" she screamed. "I want you out of my apartment and I want you to leave my key when you go." Anton took the apartment key from his pocket and threw it at her before he stormed from the apartment.

The next day Leah had her locks changed just in case there was another key. She cried herself to sleep for the next couple of nights. Heartbroken and depressed she replayed the events of her relationship with Anton over and over again. What had she missed, she wondered. Was there anything that she should have seen? When Felecia called a couple of days later Leah was still deeply depressed. Leah spoke in hushed, almost inaudible tones and Felicia could hardly hear her. "I'm coming over right now," she said.

When Leah opened the door, Felicia was shocked to see Leah is such disarray. Her hair hadn't been done in a couple of days and hung shabbily around her face. She wore a pair of old sweats and a t-shirt that was dirty and stained. "Oh my god, look at you Leah!"

Leah didn't answer. She just curled up on the end of her sofa.

"Have you eaten anything?"

"I don't feel like eating."

"You have to eat Leah. How do you feel about Chinese?"

"I don't care."

"Where do you keep your menus?"

"They're in a kitchen drawer."

Felicia called in an order to be delivered before she went to attend to her friend. She sat down beside Leah on the sofa. "What happened? I guess you confronted Anton."

"Yeah! I confronted him but I never actually asked if he was using drugs. I just asked him to tell me what was going on with him. He flew into another rage and knocked my pictures from the wall. He got so mad I thought he was going to hit me. He hit the wall instead and left a big hole in the wall."

Felicia walked to the bedroom to see the damage for herself. "Wow!" she said.

Leah was still talking when she went back into the living room. "I told him to get out and leave my key. He threw the key at me and left."

Felicia went to her friend and cuddled her in her arms. "I'm sorry Leah but you've got to get over this. Pull yourself together girl."

"I know but I just keep asking myself if there was something I should have seen. How could I choose someone on drugs and not know?"

"He fooled you honey. Don't beat yourself up over making a bad decision. We all make at least one bad decision.

Maybe we're just so desperate for a good man that we just don't look deep enough."

The two were quiet for a while, both deep in thought. Then Felicia said, "Remember that guy Eric that I dated a couple of years ago? You remember. He was really tall and kind of goofy."

"Vaguely."

"Oh come on Leah. Remember I left him in my house and came home and caught him putting on my clothes?"

"Oh that guy! Yeah, I remember him." The two roared with laughter.

"See honey. We all make those mistakes."

After they had laughed until they absolutely couldn't laugh anymore, Leah felt much better. By the time their food order came, Leah was actually hungry. They ate, laughed, and reminisced and Leah never appreciated her friendship with Felicia more. Finally, she said, "You know Felicia, I really do love him."

"If he loves you, he'll come back to you. He knows that you know now and won't accept that lifestyle. If he really loves you, sweetie, he'll get help and come back to you.

"I just realized today that I have never seen the inside of his apartment. Whenever we went to his apartment it was just to pick something up and I would wait in the car never even questioning why he never invited me inside."

"Well I guess he had something to hide."

"Let's not talk about Anton anymore. Where are we going to have dinner on Thursdays?"

"I don't know but it certainly won't be Anton's."

About a year later, Leah was walking through Old City and she noticed that Anton's Place was boarded up with a "For Sale" sign nailed to the front door. She said a silent prayer for Anton and went on her way.

It would be two years before she saw Anton again. She ran into him at an Art Show for a friend. She saw him from across the room. He nodded and she nodded back. He began to weave his way through the crowd of people. She wanted to just duck and slip away but he moved through the crowd so quickly that he was at her side in an instant. "Leah, hello."

He was still handsome, still looked ten years younger than his age and still as charming as she remembered. "Hello. What are you doing here?"

"I was invited. I know the artist."

"Really? You know James?"

"Yes, why does that surprise you?"

"I don't really know. I guess it is a little hard to believe that you two might travel in the same circles."

"Oh I see. You don't think that James could be friends with a junkie. James is too cool, too together to hang out with a coke head."

"I didn't say that."

"No, no, it's alright. I know what you think of me and you have reason to feel as you do, but I'm clean now, Leah. You were right about me. It was something that I started doing just to have fun but it took over my life. I lost you. I lost my restaurant and the respect of many friends and colleagues. But, that's all behind me now. I checked into a rehab and I've been clean for almost a year now."

"Oh, I'm so happy to hear that you've been able to get yourself together." Awkward seconds passed. "Well, it was nice seeing you again." She stuck out her hand to shake his but instead he took her hand and pulled her close to him.

"Can I see you again?"

"I'm sorry Anton. I don't think that's a good idea."

"Why not? You know you loved me Leah and I loved you. Why can't we just pick up where we left off?"

"You're right Anton. I really did love you. I thought you were the best thing to happen to me in a very long time, but you didn't love me enough to trust me. You kept things from me and when I started to think that there was a problem, you didn't trust me enough to confide in me. You wouldn't even let me help you with your problem."

"So I've made a few mistakes. It won't happen again."

"I know it won't. I'm over you, Anton. I was heartsick and it took a long time to get over you. Nevertheless, just like you, I've overcome. I am completely over you but I do wish you success and a very good life." She leaned up and placed a kiss on his cheek before turning and walking away.

Anton suddenly felt the weight of loss as he watched Leah walk out of his life forever.

BROKEN

The streets were dirty with old snow. Just hours earlier, a cold blanket of white gave the impression of a pristine city. The snow had fallen softly and silently through the night, covering everything with its light wet crystals. The snow seemed to have hushed the usual sounds of the city. Nature's beautiful covering would not last long. Once the sun rose and the city came alive again, daily life would spread the filth of human inhabitants.

A light wind pushed the storm north, leaving the air crisp and clean but extremely cold. Rasheem rose early that day in 1930. He walked east, crossing the Schuylkill Bridge at 30th

Street. His hands were balled tightly and stuffed into what was left of the pockets of his wool coat. He quickly moved through the center of the city. Usually he would stop on Market Street to grab a bite to eat for breakfast before continuing his journey toward the Delaware River. There would be no stopping this morning, as the only thing Rasheem could pull from the pockets of his trousers was lint. It seemed to him that the whole world had gone broke overnight. A couple of years earlier he'd had a good job as a chauffeur working for a family in Overbrook Farms. Besides driving the family around, he was responsible for keeping their cars clean and in good working order. Then one day his employer, Mr. Barns, took a pistol and just blew his brains out. After Mr. Barns was laid to rest, the entire staff was let go. The rumor was that Mr. Barnes had loss all of his money in the stock market. Rasheem had not been able to find a decent job since then.

Now days the Front Street dock was the only place in the city where a man could pick up a day's work. Sometimes Rasheem would be hired on to load and unload ships at the dock. In summer, he could sometimes hitch a ride across the river to pick tomatoes or apples at the Jersey orchards.

By the time Rasheem reached the river, he was so cold he could hardly move his fingers. A crowd of black men and some poor whites had already gathered in differing spots down the pier. Rasheem made his way toward the first barrel fire he saw. He stood close, holding his hands above the fire, kneading them until he felt the blood begin to circulate again.

After what seemed like hours, the crowd began to thin as men were hired on by different ship's crews. By noon, it was only Rasheem and three other men who hadn't been hired and they all knew that the hiring for the day was over. Rasheem began to make his way back home.

Dread hung on his shoulders like a heavy cloak. He hadn't worked in a couple of months now and the little bit of money his wife made was hardly enough to support his growing family. He quickly decided that he did not want to go home. He couldn't bear to see the sullen look in Anna's eyes when he told her that, once again, he hadn't made any money. Of course, Anna would not criticize him; she hardly had to say anything. It was Rasheem's own guilt and feelings of unworthiness that he imagined he saw in her eyes.

Going home at that moment was simply not an option. Instead, he went to the neighborhood speakeasy where he met some friends. They were all in similar situations and together they would express their frustrations over trying to provide for a family when there was no work and no money.

The speakeasy was a small row house on Brown Street. Once inside he sunk into a chair in the corner of the room. The weight of his own body seemed too much for him to carry and his head began to ache. The owner's name was Ed but everyone called him Hoagie. "Hey man," Hoagie said. "You look like hell. What's going on with you?"

Although Hoagie was fifteen years older than Rasheem, their unlikely friendship grew out of a mutual respect for one another. Hoagie was the older streetwise mentor, while Rasheem was a young man who began his adult life laden with the burdens of the times.

Rasheem removed his hat and stuffed it into his pocket before looking at his old friend. "I ain't got a dime to my name and I just hate to face Anna and tell her that I can't even buy supper for tonight."

Hoagie motioned for his wife to bring a bottle of gin to the table and two glasses. He sat down with Rasheem. "I can lend you some cash, if it will help, Sheem."

"That's real nice of you Hoagie, but I can't take your money, cause I don't know if I'll be able to pay you back."

"Hey man, I ain't a rich man, you know. How much you think I can afford to give away? I'm just as poor as you are but I can spare a few dollars for an old friend down on his luck. Besides, I'd like to think that you would do the same for me, if you could."

"I'm sorry, Hoagie. I didn't mean to insult you. It's just that I ain't been able to find work for a couple of months now and I just don't know what else to do. It's getting harder every day. How can a man call himself a breadwinner if he can't put a loaf of bread on his own table?" Rasheem sulked as Hoagie poured him a generous glass of gin. He tossed the drink into his mouth and swallowed hard. The liquid seemed to burn a path to his stomach, warming him inside and out. Hoagie poured another glass and Rasheem drank again.

"You know Hoagie, I see more and more white boys on them docks in the morning. There was a time when they wouldn't be caught dead doing days' work, but since a lot of them loss their jobs too, they're taking all the jobs at the docks. When the crew chiefs come down to pick a crew, they pick the white boys first. We ain't got a chance and I just don't know what else to do." Hoagie didn't answer but he knew what Rasheem was going through.

It was near seven in the evening when Rasheem stumbled from Hoagie's place and started for home. It was bitterly cold but Rasheem was still warmed by the liquor he'd consumed and he was too drunk to notice how cold it had become. He made his way home, stumbling and sliding on the ice covered sidewalks until he reached his door. He and Anna had rented a small house on Brooklyn Street. At first, it had been just the two of them, but Anna's mother, Louise, lost her job and had moved in with them about a year ago. Soon after that, his younger brother needed a place to stay. Lawrence had assured Rasheem and Anna that he would only need to stay until he could get his own place, but with work being so scarce, no one knew when he would be able to move out. Rasheem had a full house and no one had a job except his wife. If that wasn't enough trouble to bear, Anna was pregnant and expected to deliver in only a couple of months.

They lived off the scraps Anna was allowed to take from the home of the white family she worked for in Wynnefield Heights. Rasheem knew that his situation became direr with every passing day.

As he fumbled with his key in the front door, the door was suddenly yanked open and Louise stood there with her anger clearly etched in the lines of her face. She looked down at Rasheem, her brows furrowed together. "What kind of a husband are you to keep your wife here worrying about you all day, while you are somewhere drinking yourself into a stupor?"

As Rasheem looked up into his mother-in-law's hate filled eyes, his alcoholic euphoria began to slowly slip away. He wanted to remind Louise that it was his door that she'd opened and that she could leave whenever the mood suited her; but he knew that such disrespect would not be tolerated by Anna. Instead, he took his forearm and pushed his mother-in-law aside before he walked into his house. Louise was close on his heels.

Anna sat in a chair facing the front window. Rasheem guessed that she had probably been sitting in that same position for most of the afternoon. Her skillful fingers worked her yarn and knitting needles at an astounding pace, creating a blue and pink baby blanket. She did not, at first, look up from her task. "There's a plate in the stove for you, honey," she said.

"I'm not hungry."

"Have you already eaten?"

"No. He probably just drank his supper," Louise put in.

Rasheem rolled his eyes toward his mother-in-law. "No Anna. I'm just not hungry."

"Too full of that poison," Louise antagonized.

"Louise!" Rasheem tried to keep an even tone. "Anna and I are trying to have a discussion. We would like to have at least one conversation without you butting into it."

"Now you listen to me," Louise was more than ready for an argument as she put her hands on her hips and slid up to Rasheem. "I ain't gone take no more sass talk from you Rasheem. I'll . . ."

"Mother, please," was all Anna had to say to put an end to the verbal squabble. Unable to hide her annoyance, Louise slammed the front door closed and marched up to her bedroom.

Rasheem sat on the sofa across from his wife, eyeing her suspiciously. He knew that Anna was trying to put on a brave face, but he also knew that she was disappointed in him. Her smile was forced but her eyes held the sadness her smile tried to hide. Oh how he wished to see a genuine smile on that pretty face. He wanted to reassure her but how could he when he had loss hope. "Anna," he said. Then overcome with emotion he fell to his knees and crawled to her, laying his head in her lap. She dropped her knitting and began to caresses his head, trying to comfort him. The two were quiet for a few minutes. "Anna, I'm sorry," he finally whispered.

"What exactly are you sorry for, Rasheem? Are you sorry that you have a family that depends on you or that your wife is expecting to deliver your first child soon?"

"No! No!" Rasheem said as he jumped to his feet. "You know that isn't it, Anna. I love you with all of my heart."

"Then what, Rasheem? There is nothing for you to be sorry for Rasheem. You are not the only man having a difficult time right now."

Rasheem stood up and walked thoughtfully before the front window with his hands in his pockets. They were silent for a while. Evening became night and the living room grew dim. Anna put away her knitting and watched her husband wishing she could read his mind or at least say something to ease his pain. Finally, she said, "I'm sorry too, Rasheem."

"You?" Rasheem turned to face Anna again. "What could you possibly be sorry about?"

"I'm sorry that you felt the need to get drunk instead of coming home and talking with me about all of this." Feeling like a broken man, Rasheem returned his head to his wife's lap and cried like a baby.

Lawrence had been huddled close to the radio in the dining room when he heard his big brother sobbing. He got up and slowly walked to the archway between the two rooms and stood watching the scene before him. He grew up in the shadow of his perfect big brother, seeing Rasheem as his hero and the one destined for success. Rasheem's tears did not immediately diminish him in his brother's eyes, because Lawrence could not, at first, believe what he was seeing.

Anna returned her hand to her husband's head, consoling him and caressing him as she would a small child. With her other hand she motioned for Lawrence to leave. She hoped that he would understand that she and Rasheem needed time alone.

She told her husband that everything would be all right and that he need not worry because she was sure that God would bless and keep them. Later, she prayed, appealing to God to intervene in their situation.

"I'm sorry, Anna," Rasheem said again.

"I know honey."

"I just didn't want to come home empty handed again, and tell you that I couldn't find work."

"Rasheem, no one can find work. Don't you read the papers? The country is in a depression. I'm not sure exactly what that means but I hear the Fords talking about it all of the time. Banks are closing and big companies are going broke. The Fords have already let some of the house staffs go and any day now, the Fords might let the rest of the staff go. They're almost as broke as everyone else."

"Anna, what are we going to do if you lose work too?" He placed his hand over her bulging belly. "What are we going to do?" he asked again. "Every day that I walk downtown, I pass bread lines that are sometimes blocks long. Whites and blacks are standing in the same line, waiting to get free government food. I can't bear the thought of standing in one of those lines."

"Don't think about it Sheem. We will just keep going as we have. You have to have faith, honey. Something will change. You'll see."

The next day was the same as all the other days that came before that day. Rasheem stayed at the docks until well after noon before he gave up and headed for home. Again, he stopped at Hoagie's speakeasy. He promised himself that he would only have one drink and then he would go straight home.

Hoagie's was becoming more and more crowded as more neighborhood men found themselves without jobs and nothing to do in the afternoons. Hoagie, Rasheem and a few other neighbors sat around the table discussing what the papers were calling, The Great Depression. "I never thought I'd see the day when rich people in this country were brought low," Hoagie said.

"Me neither," one of the other men said. "I was working at the Dixon Paper Box Factory. One morning when we all clocked in for work, someone found Mr. Dixon dead in his office. They say he shot himself. I can't understand why he would go and do a fool thing like that."

"It ain't hard to figure," Hoagie said as he refilled the glasses with new gin. "Some of those white folks been rich for generations. They don't know how to live poor. We on the other hand, always been poor. Oh yeah, sometimes are better than others, but we know how to make due during the lean times."

All four men were quiet for a time, each contemplating the words of their wise old friend. "We know how to make due," were the words that played repeatedly in Rasheem's head. How could he make due?

"Well, I'd better be going," Bill said, as he threw a crumpled dollar on the table."

"Me too," the other man said.

Rasheem stood up to leave too. "Hold on Sheem," Hoagie said. "I want to talk to you a minute."

When the others had left, Hoagie sat down with Sheem. "I might be able to help you with your particular situation, Rahseem."

"Yeah? How?"

"I got a friend that needs a driver. Think you can drive a truck."

"Sure. Where does he want me to drive?"

"Well, this friend needs someone to deliver a shipment. You don't even have to leave the city. All you have to do is go down to the docks, like you do every morning. There will be a pickup truck already loaded with the shipment."

Rasheem became a little suspicious. "You sound kind of mysterious, Hoagie. Just what is this friend shipping?"

"Look Sheem, I'm offering you a way to make some money, pay your bills. For god's sake man, I'm offering you a way to put food on your table. You gonna turn that down?"

Rasheem thought for a few minutes. He didn't like the thought of Anna on her knees, scrubbing the floors in her seventh month of pregnancy with hardly enough food in her belly to nourish her, let alone her baby. "Alright," he said slowly. "Tell me more."

"All you have to do is get into the truck. The keys will already be there. You drive the truck to a warehouse downtown and park. You don't even have to unload the shipment. You'll find an envelope on the seat with the delivery address and five crisp one hundred dollar bills. Now, with two or more deliveries a week, you'll be almost a rich man."

"Wow! Five hundred dollars? Must be a really important shipment."

Hoagie just laughed.

A week later, the Sears store delivered a new baby crib to the Brown house on Brooklyn Street. Louise and Anna thought that someone at the Sears store must have made a grave mistake. The delivery man was at the door trying to convince Anna that the crib had been bought and paid for and that their house was indeed the correct delivery address.

"Look lady," the frustrated deliveryman said. "I don't much care what you do with this baby crib. My orders are to deliver the crib so I'm going to leave it right here on the curb." He and another man moved the large box from the back of the truck and deposited it on the curb in front of the house.

An hour later Rasheem came home with a shopping bag full of food in each hand and a broad smile across his face. Once inside the house he kissed Anna and handed the bags to his mother-in-law. "Hey, why didn't they bring the crib inside?"

"Oh, you know about the crib?" Louise asked.

"Know about it? I bought it," Rasheem said proudly.
He called for Lawrence to help him carry the crib indoors.

"Ute-oh!" Louise said. She began to shake her head as
if she suddenly knew the answers to unspoken questions. Anna
was silent but she stared at Rasheem in disbelief.

"Why are you all staring at me?" They all had
questions but no one asked them.

Supper was good that night. The smell of roasted
chicken, collard greens and biscuits filled the little house. A
load of coal had been delivered earlier and the house was warm
and cozy.

Anna sat knitting while Lawrence was huddled around
the radio as usual. Louise was busy in the kitchen while
Rasheem assembled the crib in the baby's room on the third
floor.

The next day Rasheem made another delivery and was
paid for his services. He thought that this was the sweetest deal
in the world. For the next three months Rasheem made the trip
at least twice a week just as Hoagie promised. Rasheem felt so
good to finally, be able to provide for his family that he hardly
thought about what he was delivering anymore. In April 1932,
Anna delivered a healthy baby girl at home who she named,
Kira Marie Brown. Rasheem was proud to be able to buy Kira
everything she needed even before her birth.

Nevertheless, later that month Rasheem began to have
trepidations. How long would this good fortune last, he
wondered. He stopped in to see Hoagie, thinking that after
making the shipments for couple of months, Hoagie might be
willing to share additional information. They greeted each other
warmly.

"Hey man," Rasheem began. "I have to thank you for
hooking me up with this gig. It's as sweet as they come."

"No need to thank me, man."

"You never told me exactly what is in those shipments."

"Well now," Hoagie scratched at his beard. "There's a reason for that Rasheem. What you don't know, you can't tell. Besides, sometimes it's better not to know something." Hoagie stood up and walked a few paces away from Rasheem. "You're being paid good money, right?"

Rasheem nodded as if he understood but he was suddenly filled with a sense of foreboding.

Rasheem made two more shipments that week but this time, as he had a few times before, he didn't go right out and spend the money. He took the fifteen hundred dollars and hid it in the floorboards of his and Anna's bedroom. The next Monday he made his way to the docks as usual but this day he could not shake the feeling that something was amiss.

The truck was parked in its usual place but today, there were a couple of guys hanging around the truck. The docks were always crowded in the morning but those two guys looked out of place. Most of the men wore work clothes while the two strangers wore suits and overcoats.

Rasheem did not approach the truck but hung around the docks as if he were trying to be hired on by a ship's crew as he had done previously. Finally, overwhelmed with curiosity and not wanting to pass up a payday, he approached the two men. "Morning," he said cheerfully but got no answer. Rasheem pulled a cigarette from his coat pocket. "Got a light?" he asked.

The man let out a long sigh making his annoyance known before he pulled his overcoat aside to retrieve his Zippo. The silver badge on his breast pocket told Rasheem that he was law enforcement. The pistol tucked in the shoulder holster under his left arm let Rasheem know that he was on the job and here to take someone down.

The man flicked his silver Zippo and the flame leaped up. Rasheem leaned down to light his cigarette while keeping his eye on the man. "Thanks," he said then slowly moved away. "Have a nice day," Rasheem said but again, did not receive a reply.

It was near ten in the morning and Rasheem wanted to leave but didn't want to call attention to himself. An hour later, the men were still waiting near the truck and there were only three men waiting at the docks. Besides Rasheem and another Negro, one white boy hadn't been hired on by a crew. A crew chief appeared with a clipboard and pencil. Rasheem was sure that the white boy would be hired but to his surprise, the man hired all three of them.

For the next six hours, Rasheem worked loading cargo on an outgoing ship. Every so often, he was able to get a glimpse of the truck parked in its usual spot. At the end of the shift, the crew chief approached Rasheem. "What's your name fellow?"

"Rasheem Brown."

"I like the way you work. You don't say much, you just work and I like that."

"Thank you, sir."

"If you can get here by five in the morning, you got yourself a job."

"Thank you. I'll be here at five on the dot."

When Rasheem left the ship, he saw that the docks were filled with federal agents and Philadelphia police. They had raided a warehouse and were arresting several men. The cargo from the truck was being loaded into another truck with a federal seal on the door. Rasheem stood and watched with the other spectators who had gathered along the pier before he slowly moved away and headed for home.

He couldn't wait to get to Hoagie's to tell him what happened. He reached Hoagie's speakeasy just in time to see him being placed in a police car with his hands cuffed behind him. They spoke no words but their eyes met. A slight nod of the head told Rasheem to keep walking. The next day, Rasheem reported to his new job promptly at five. It was hard, backbreaking work and the pay was only a miniscule of the money he made driving that truck, but the joy of not having to worry about your freedom being at stake made the job worth the hard work.

A few days later Rasheem read that a warehouse involved in the illegal shipments of whiskey was raided by federal agents. Less than a year later, February 20, 1933 Prohibition Laws were repealed and by Kira's first birthday, Rasheem's friend Hoagie was home.

Rasheem went to see Hoagie as soon as he learned that he was home. "Now you understand why I couldn't tell you what was in those shipments, right?" Hoagie asked. "Sometimes it's better just not to know everything." He laughed.

"Yeah, but I still would have liked to know."

"Why? It helped you and your family out, didn't it?"

"Yeah." They both laughed. "Like I said, it was the sweetest deal in the world."

Rasheem caught Hoagie up on neighborhood news and they laughed and talked for a while before Rasheem noticed a somber expression on his friend's face. "Hey, what's the matter Hoagie? You should be happy. You're finally home."

"Yeah, I am happy about being home but you know that I'm out of business. What am I going to do to support my family? I'm too old for the docks."

To Hoagie's surprise, Rasheem began to laugh. It was a robust bend over and slap your thigh laugh. At first Hoagie smiled too, but after a minute his face contorted in anger.

"What the hell is so funny?"

"Oh, I'm sorry," Rasheem said trying to calm himself. "I guess I should have told you this right off, but I was so happy to see you that it slipped my mind."

"What! Spill it Sheem!"

"Well," Rasheem smiled trying to prolong the moment. "You aren't exactly out of business, man. In fact, you and I will be going into a brand new business."

Hoagie eyed Rasheem suspiciously.

"Remember those delivers I made to the warehouse?"

"Yeah, what of it?"

"Well, I saved a good bit of that money, almost ten thousand dollars."

"You're kidding, right?"

"Nope. I've got enough for us to open up our own bar."

"You're kidding, right?" Hoagie said again.

"No, I'm telling you the truth. I've already bought a place and started renovating. It's on Market Street, just this side of the river. Come on, I'll show it to you."

Rasheem had also been able to buy a used car and together they rode the few blocks to the bar. As soon as the car was parked, the two men got out and stood at the curb looking up at their new business. The façade was red brick with a large plate glass window that had been painted black with large box letters in white, trimmed in light blue that read, HOAGIE'S NITE SPOT.

"The entire time you were in prison, all I could think about was how I could pay you back for what you did for me and my family."

"Thank you, Sheem. You are a good man and a good friend."

PASSING

At sixteen racism was something that I'd only read about. Of course, I knew that people had their particular prejudices but racism just wasn't a part of the world in which I lived. That would change suddenly and unceremoniously when while working in an ice cream parlor, a young white woman refused to have me serve her. Though it was the middle of July, the weather was unusually cool and customers weren't exactly standing in line for a cold treat. The manager decided that we should close the store early but the lady came in with two small children just as we were closing.

"Can I help you," I said a little too eager. I guess I was just grateful for a chance to do something other than wiping the counter for the tenth time.

"No," she said bluntly. She didn't bother to offer an explanation but turned her attention away from me as if I'd been dismissed.

"But you're the only one here," I said without hiding my confusion.

"Is there someone else besides you working today?" she asked curtly.

"Only the manager."

"Fine, may I see the manager, please?"

This lady wasn't the first customer I'd served who had been less than pleasant but this was different. Her hostility seemed to be directed at me personally though I didn't know her and couldn't have offended her in any way.

I went to the back of the store and returned a few minutes later with the manager Mr. Harris. He was a tall soft-spoken part-time seminary student who just happened to be white. "Is there a problem?" he asked.

"No," the customer said then she proceeded to order three cones of ice cream in varying flavors. Mr. Harris looked just as confused as I was and he didn't move to fill her order right away. Uncomfortable seconds passed.

"Mia," he said to me. "Would you take this customer's order please?"

"I would really prefer you to dip my ice cream," she said before I could answer. "If that's a problem I'll come back another time."

"Why?" Mr. Harris asked.

"Well, because she's black," she replied as if her explanation was not only valid but also obvious. Mr. Harris and I were both dumbfounded as we stood staring at the woman.

Mr. Harris did fill her order in his usual pleasant manner. Afterwards we both laughed finding the entire incident like something right out of the nineteen sixties. "I didn't know people like her still existed," Mr. Harris said.

What Mr. Harris couldn't know was that the incident would be the catalyst that would awaken in me a desire to know myself. I know that sounds ridiculous since most people grow up with a good sense self, but at that point I really didn't know myself. I didn't think of myself as black. I was biracial, a fact that I assumed was as evident as the color of my eyes. Now I wondered if other people saw me as black and if so why didn't I feel like a black person?

I grew up in a multiracial suburb of Philadelphia where race was never an issue. My friends were Black, White, Asian, and Hispanic. Some of my friends were Jewish, Christian and Muslim and it had never made the slightest difference to any of us. Until that day, my parents had just been my parents. Now I saw them as my white father and my black mother.

The first person I mentioned the incident to was my older brother but he had no advice for me. I assumed that because he looked "whiter" than I did, he'd probably never encountered anything remotely similar to what I had experienced. "Screw her," was his response.

Finally, I told my mother about the incident. "Were you offended?" she wanted to know.

"I'm not sure. At first, I thought the lady was just silly, we even laughed about the whole thing. It wasn't until it was all over that I started to really think about it."

"Are you offended now?"

"Why should I be offended? I'm not black, at least not all black."

"If you thought of yourself as black instead of biracial you would certainly have been offended and you would have known right away that the woman's comments were racially motivated." I could hear the agitation in my mother's voice.

"Why are you angry?" I asked.

"I'm not angry. I guess I've always known that we would one day have this conversation but I figured you would be much older and the world would have changed at least a little by the time we would have to talk about this." She leaned back on the patio lounge chair, visibly taking a deep breath. "Mia," she said softly. "In this country you will always be considered black."

"But I'm not black," I protested. "How can I be black when my father is white?"

"In this country one ounce of black blood makes you black."

"I don't understand."

"During the times when Africans were enslaved in this country if a child was born to a black woman, even if that child was fathered by a white man, the child was considered black. It's the one-ounce rule. Because we were considered chattel, believing that one ounce of black blood made the child black, allowed slave owners to increase their wealth. The more slaves a planter owned the more hands in the fields, which made for a larger harvest and more profit. They were so greedy they would even sell their own sons and daughters."

"But Mom, people don't still believe that, do they?"

"I would like to think that people are more open-minded these days but there will always be some people who won't or can't look beyond race. That doesn't mean that you should ever be ashamed of who you are no matter what some closed-minded bigot says to you. Do you understand?"

"Yeah, I think so. When you really think about it, if the blood of the African is so dominant as to override any other races, there must be millions of us out there that no one even knows about."

"You're right. The old folks call that passing. There are a lot of blacks who were light enough to pass for white and it's been going on for more than a hundred years."

My mother's words were meant to explain and console but they only confused me more. For the next couple of years, I shied away from the subject as much as I could. It would not surface again until my second year in college.

I signed up for a class in African American Studies hoping to learn a little more than the information I learned from public television documentaries. Before I knew it, I was in the middle of a sea of dread locs, braids, head wraps of every imaginable pattern and women with their heads shaved. Some of the men wore black t-shirts with slogans like, KILL WHITEY or BLACK POWER. Some of them wore shirts with a picture of Malcolm X or Huey Newton on the front. I didn't even know who Huey Newton was until someone explained to me that he was one of the founding members of the Black Panther Party.

At first, I felt as if I were an alien visiting another world. The atmosphere in our class was sometimes tense and it seemed to me that some of the students expressed their blackness with a hostility and belligerence that I couldn't understand. Everything around me was foreign.

Some of the students addressed me as, "the white girl." Other students wanted to know what I was as if I were of a completely different species. "You Puerto Rican or something?" Still others only wanted to know my name. What was even stranger to me was, when I told my classmates that I was biracial, they seemed to disregard my one white parent. I was immediately accepted which told me that the one-drop rule was a concept that even blacks believed.

Some of us spent time after classes and on weekends going to poetry readings and rap sessions at coffee houses and pubs. I felt as if I was growing and the more I learned the more mesmerized I became. I wanted nothing more than to get in touch with my blackness, to celebrate my roots and wear my newfound identity as a patriot waves a flag.

I went to a Loctician who assured me that with time and patience she could transform my long straight auburn hair into coiled locs.

The gold pendant that my father had given me for my eighteenth birthday was locked away in my jewelry case and I proudly wore cowry shells and handmade silver and jade earrings and necklaces. My cardigan sweaters and wool slacks were packed in cardboard boxes sprinkled with moth crystals and I began to wear cotton slacks, Dashikis, and Kente Cloth dresses with sandals. I read books and poetry by Maya Angelou, James Baldwin, Richard Wright, and Na'im Akbar. When I learned that the cradle of civilization began in Africa, I felt vindicated. I strutted around the campus as a proud black woman. My new friends no longer called me white girl. They called me Sista and I loved it.

On some of my visits home, I noticed that some of the people I had grown up with stared at me and whispered to one another behind my back. My mother, although a little shocked, did nothing to discourage me. My father told me I looked foolish and that my clothes were like a bad Halloween costume. I was twenty years old then and like most twenty year olds, I had more idealism than common sense. I reasoned that if my father did not like my clothes, he did not like me. I thought I had it all figured out but in truth my learning had just begun.

Because my hair is naturally straight, a characteristic obviously inherited from my white ancestors, my visits to my Loctician, Kadeshia, were frequent. On one of those visits Kadeshia said, "Why are you so determined to wear locs when your natural hair is so pretty?"

Her question stunned me. How could this beautiful black woman think that my straight hair was pretty? "I wear my locs to celebrate my blackness," I said proudly. "My locs are beautiful. Isn't that why anyone wears locs?"

"Does that mean that you don't celebrate your whiteness?"

"What?" For the past two years, I hadn't even acknowledged that there was even the slightest measure of

Caucasian in my bloodline. I didn't know how to answer
Kadeshia.

"If you ask me sista, you are not being true to yourself.
You are a beautiful mixture of the races but you are trying to
pass for black."

"No I'm not, my mother is Black."

"And your father is White. Are you ashamed of that
fact?"

"No. I have no reason to be ashamed of anything," I
said defensively.

"Then Sista, you should ask yourself why you feel the
need to align yourself with one or the other?"

I sat quietly for a few moments as Kadeshia softly
palm rolled my straight hair into coils. Was I really just passing
for black, I wondered. It was true that none of this had actually
come naturally to me. I had forced myself into a world where I
didn't exactly fit. It was like wedging a round peg into a square
opening, with some pressure you could get it in but there would
always be gaping spaces around the peg.

Kadeshia's off-handed comments made me again
question my identity. Although I know that it wasn't her
intention, the word "passing" offended me. To say that I was
merely "passing" meant that I was a fake, an imitation of the
real thing. I never wanted to be anything but my true self. I
wanted to identify with my people or at least who I thought
were my people. Kadeshia made me realize that my people
were both black and white.

That evening I called my father to first apologize for
shutting him out of my life, and second for neglecting to
acknowledge that he was as much a part of me as my mother.
He told me that he hadn't taken offense and that he knew that
this was something I would have to work through on my own.

Two weeks later, I went home for a visit and my parents took my brother and me to Rochester to meet our aging Italian grandmother. She readily admitted that she and her family hadn't been too happy when my parents married.

"That's all water under the bridge now," she said. "I'm too old to hold grudges, dear. Now come and give your grandmother a hug. We've got a lot of making up to do." That weekend I was introduced to my family. Some of my relatives lived close to my grandmother and came to visit after she called them. We spent the entire weekend getting to know one another and looking at old photos while Grandmother tried to remember the stories that went with each photo. We left promising to visit more often.

It was a weekend that I will never forget. I came away feeling as if the weight of the world had been lifted from my shoulders. I felt free in a way that I'd never felt before. I was free to just be myself.

Slowly and without effort or forethought, many of the trappings of my misguided afro-centrism began to fall away but I have to admit, I do love my locs.

WRONG SIDE OF TOWN

Jane seems happy to hear that Laurence and I have decided to marry. I wasn't sure how she would react to the prospect of losing her only son. It seemed as though we had taken an instant dislike for one another even though we hadn't spent more than a few minutes together on only a few occasions. Even before we'd shared our plans with his family, Jane treated me as if I'd stolen something from her. I really didn't think of it as odd, but she made me feel a little uncomfortable. After all, Laurence was Jane's only son and I was well aware of the special relationship my fiancé had with his mother. Laurence loss his father when he was very young and for most of his life, it was just the two of them. He was the man in Jane's life and she depended on him a great deal. Knowing all of this, I would not want to do anything to displease Jane. After Laurence announced our plans, he thought it might be a good idea for me to spend a little more time with his mother. He wanted his mother and me to get along more than anything. I promised that I'd do my best to win his mother's respect if not her blessing.

However, there was something very different about today. She was genuinely nice to me and I felt even more ill at ease than I did before. There we sat on the veranda overlooking the city and having tea and polite conversation. "I suppose you'll want to move out of that tiny little apartment in the city as quickly as possible?" Jane said.

"No. As a matter of fact, Laurence and I were considering keeping the apartment after we've married." I tried to keep my voice even and not reveal my agitation.

"Whatever for?" Jane said in her most snobbish voice. A couple of years ago I didn't even know that African Americans could be snobbish. Meeting Laurence's family had given me a glimpse into a part of the African American community that I didn't even know existed. Jane's family had money, old money. Her grandfather had been one of the first African Americans to graduate from the University of Pennsylvania as an engineer. The wealth that he accumulated over his eighty years enabled his family to continue to rise. Jane had inherited a fortune along with her Lafayette Hills mansion.

"Well," I stammered. "The apartment is close to my office in the city and Laurence and I love being in the city."

"But of course you'll be giving up that dreadful office job after you and Laurence have married."

I wasn't sure if that was a question or a demand. "Jane, I never planned to quit my job."

"Well, you should consider it. After all, Laurence will want you at home to devote your time to the many social and charitable obligations that will become your duty as Mrs. Laurence Kennis."

"You don't know your son as well as you might think, Jane. Laurence has no problem with me working."

"Well of course he didn't. An unmarried girl in your situation must support herself somehow. However, after you've married there will be no reason to spend that much time away from your home."

I took a sip of tea and swallowed slowly. Choosing my words carefully I said, "Jane, let's not play word games here. I know that you would rather someone else become Mrs. Laurence Kennis but quite frankly, it isn't your decision to make. I also know that you don't like me very much but I know that's because you don't really know me."

"What is there to know, dear? I know that you've never had much of anything and you think that by marring my son you'll have everything. Do you really think I need to know any more than that?"

Although we were well outside of the Philadelphia, from her veranda I could see the bright lights of the entire city. William Penn loomed in the distance with his back to me and the Schuylkill looked like a piece of yarn winding through a model city. I inhaled gulps of fresh air trying to clear my head and cool my temper. Maybe Jane was right, I thought. I could never fit into this family. I came from a family where we were

taught that the struggle of all Africans was our struggle, a
unified struggle and we empathized with Africans around the
globe, no matter what their station in life. Maybe Laurence
would be better off with someone from his background. All of
these things ran through my head as I looked at the woman who
would soon be my mother-in-law.

    She sat there with her spine stiff and unyielding. Her
steel gray hair pulled back into a bun at the nape of her neck.
Diamond studs graced her ears and her fingers were jeweled
with diamonds and rubies. Does this woman even know that she
is a black woman, I wondered. She believes that her money
gives her the right to look down her snobbish nose at me. I
wanted to give up, give in and say the hell with it all. For
reasons I will never understand I did not give up but said,
"That's not fair Jane."

    Her hazel eyes brightened in surprise. Maybe it was my
tone rather than my words but at that moment, I could feel that
we'd made a break through. "You're judging my character by
where I come from. I'm not ashamed of my background Jane.
Yes, I was born and raised in West Philadelphia and my parents
worked very hard to send my sister and me to college. They
taught us values and manners. You don't have to be born with a
silver spoon in your mouth to be a good person."

    "I never said . . ."

    "I'm not finished," I said cutting short whatever it was
she wanted to say. "I am a good person in spite of what you
believe. Your son loves me because he knows that I am a good
person. Your money doesn't impress me Jane. The only thing I
want from Laurence is his love and respect." I couldn't believe
I was sitting here defending myself when I've done nothing
wrong. Angry with myself for letting her goad me into this
verbal confrontation, I stood and walked over to the railing and
turned my back to Jane.

"I think that we have misunderstood each other Terri. Let me set things straight so that we can end this ridiculous conversation." That was the first time I heard Jane use my name instead of her condescending, "dear."

"I have nothing against you Terri. I just don't think that you're the right girl for my son. That is my opinion, right or wrong." There was the usual hint of sarcasm in her voice.

I knew that I would never win her over and at that moment, I no longer cared to try. I was from the wrong side of town and as long as I was unable to change that fact, she would never consider me a suitable wife for Laurence. Because I no longer cared, I felt free to say what I felt because it no longer mattered if Jane liked me or not. I took my seat again and leaned forward so I could look Jane in the eye as I spoke.

"Laurence has grown up with the right girls, Jane. He's been around the right kind of girls all of his life. You've introduced him to all the right girls that he may not have known but he didn't fall in love with any of them. He loves me whether you approve or not, he still loves me."

Jane leaned back in her chair as if she needed time to process this new information. She took a long sip of tea and replaced her teacup on its saucer with a clang. I expected reproach or anger but Jane was unperturbed. I had the strangest feeling that we had come to some sort of turning point. She smiled at me and folded her hands, resting them on the edge of the table. "Well, my dear. That is the first thing you've said to which I agree. Laurence does love you though I hardly see why."

I relaxed. "I'll be a good wife to Laurence because I love him as much as he loves me."

"That," she said shaking a finger at me, "remains to be seen." Once again she managed to silence me with a few biting words. I sat back in my chair wondering what would come next.

"Terri, I think we are beginning to understand each other. Let me clarify my position as well as your own in this situation. As I said, I don't think that you will make a proper wife for my son but that remains to be seen. The most important thing in this world to me is my son's happiness. Do you understand dear?" She didn't wait for a response. "You make Laurence happy and I can't deny that fact. It doesn't matter if I approve of this marriage. What does matter is that I approve of my son's happiness. As long as you remember that Laurence's happiness is my first concern, we'll get along just fine."

THE DAY LITTLE AFRICA BURNED

What I remember most about that horrific day is fire. I was twelve years old the day little Africa burned. Most of what was loss that day will be mourned forever. In the events of that day, I lost an Aunt, two cousins and my very best friend. It was May 31, 1921, a day that no one who was there would ever forget. The memory is as much of part of me as my own skin. It doesn't change or fade and it doesn't slip in and out like a dream. Whether in the middle of the afternoon when I'm wide awake, or in the dead of night when I'm fast asleep, I can still see the fire, feel its heat on my face, hear the screams and smell the stench of people being burned alive.

We lived in Greenwood, a little section of Tulsa, Oklahoma folks called, "Little Africa." In those days, everything was segregated and Black people were shut out of much of the city of Tula. Segregation caused them to band together as an independent community. The black people of Greenwood built their own libraries, theaters, banks, schools, and many businesses. They became so prosperous in their own right that some people began to call Greenwood "The Black Wall Street."

My father, Frank, owned the shoe repair shop. The front of our house was a storefront where my daddy repaired shoes. We lived in the back and on the two floors above. There was my mother Marie, my baby sister Frances, my Father and me. Leann, my best friend and classmate, lived right next door. The front of her house was a storefront too, where her family sold produce.

It was a warm spring evening and my father walked us kids down the block to buy ice cream cones. On the way back, we laughed and talked while enjoying our ice cream and the warm weather. My father stopped along the way to greet neighbors as we walked. "Hey Joe," he said. "How's it going?"

"Oh, I can't complain. Another day, another dollar; ain't that how it goes, Frank?"

"Well, I guess that depends. Some folks just get another trouble." The two men laughed as they shook hands.

A little further, down the block we saw another neighbor. It was Mr. Jake from the church. "Hey Frank, you seen the paper today?" he asked. Mr. Jake seemed agitated.

"No," Daddy said. "What's up?"

"This here paper says that Richard raped a white woman."

"No. You don't mean Dick Rowland?" I watched as the color drained from my father's face.

"Yep! That's what it says."

"That's a lie," Daddy said. "I talked to him just yesterday and he told me the whole story. He works in the Drexel building downtown shining shoes. He told me that he just touched that white woman on her arm and she went crazy. He was trying to tell her something but he didn't get a word in edgewise. He said that she just started screaming as if he was gonna killer her. He backed away from her and she just started whacking him about the head until he just ran away."

"That may be what he told you but it says here," Mr. Jake pointed to the newspaper he held in his hand, "that she went right to the sheriff and reported that he attacked her. They arrested Dick yesterday afternoon."

We had stopped walking and the ice cream cone that my father held had begun to melt. Cold white cream ran down his arm in streaks as he stood there on the sidewalk and considered what Mr. Jake said. Time seemed to stop as we all stood watching my father's smile transform into a straight line of concern. "Are you sure, Jake?"

"Yeah! Willie says that the whites are gonna break Dick out of jail and lynch him. They're forming a lynch mob right now, down at the courthouse."

"Oh no! I hope you're wrong about this Jake, but I think we best be getting over to the courthouse and see if we can stop this thing before it gets out of hand. Let me take the girls home. I'll meet you in front of the shoe shop in five minutes."

"I'll get some of the men from the church to go with us," Mr. Jake said.

"No!" Daddy said. He threw his melted ice cream in a waste can. "It won't do any good for us to look like a mob. Just the two of us may be able to talk the Sheriff into preventing any trouble."

With that, he began to walk briskly down the block, pulling Frances behind him. The joys of that spring evening came to an end. He walked Leann to her front door and explained to her parents about the lynch mob at the courthouse. When we got to our house, he told my mother about the gathering mob. We all watched in confusion as he pushed our china cabinet away from its place against the wall. Then he reached behind the cabinet and pulled out a revolver that had been taped to the back of the cabinet.

"Oh my God!" My mother said when she saw the gun. "Frank no! You can't go trying to stop a mob with that thing. They'll string you up right next to Dick Rowland."

Daddy's expression was still grim as he glanced at Mother but did not answer her. He pulled a box of bullets from one of the cabinet drawers and began to load his revolver.

My mother ran to the other side of the table, trying to appeal to my father not to go. "Frank, this is not our fight."

"Why ain't it?"

"Because Frank, we have nothing to do with this. You don't know what this Dick did or didn't do."

"That's just it Marie, I do know. I know this man. I've known him for years and I know that he wouldn't do such a thing."

"What if something happens to you? What are we supposed to do?"

"You ever seen a lynch mob, Marie?"

"No."

"Well I have, and I know that if we don't stop this thing before it gets out of hand, we will all be in danger. "

My mother started to cry softly and my sister ran to her, smothering her own cries in mother's skirt.

"Don't worry Marie," my father said as he pushed the gun into his trousers and pulled on a jacket to hide it. "I just want to see that Dick gets a fair trial."

"What makes you think any of them white people will listen to you," she said through her sobs.

My father's face had a strange expression. It was mixture of determination and fear as he ignored my mother's protest again and walked to our front door. "Lock this door when I'm gone and you and the girls wait for me upstairs."

My mother did as my father said and ushered Frances and me to our upstairs parlor. Though I could see that my parents were afraid, I could not understand what it was exactly that they feared. I tried to read while my sister Frances busied herself cradling her baby doll. My mother paced the short distance between our sofa and the far wall of the small room. Back and forth she walked as she twisted and wrung her hands together in worry.

I'm not sure just how long we stayed upstairs before all hell broke loose. Suddenly there were loud voices in the street below and we all ran to the window to see what was happening. To this day, I am still haunted by what we saw there in the street. My mother turned off all of the lamps except a single candle that burned in a wall scone in the hall.

As the three of us stood there watching the chaos that had erupted in our street, we saw Mr. Jefferies, Leann's father, run into the street to help an old man who had fallen in his haste to flee the growing mob. Four white men appeared, swooping Mr. Jefferies off of his feet. He fought them, swinging his fist and kicking his feet. However, he could not free himself from the murderous clutches of his captors. A noose was quickly slipped over his head and in seconds, he was hung from the same iron beam that held the shingle for his produce store.

Crazed with bigotry and hatred, the white people were destroying everything in their path. Some of them were running down Archer Street with torches and guns, screaming, shouting, and shooting at every black person they came across. My mother tried to move us away from the window but I was transfixed. Frances began to cry, covering her eyes and backing away from the window. My mother grabbed Frances by the arm and pulled her away. She then began to scream at me. "Denise! Denise! Come here. We've got to go, honey. It's not safe here anymore." Just then we heard a loud boom, the house trembled from the blast and suddenly it seemed as if the whole world was on fire.

Pickup trucks were filled with men carrying guns and torches. Some held ropes that had already been tied into nooses for hanging. Others were on horseback, trampling and ransacking every house and business on Archer Street.

There was a storm cellar under our house where my mother thought we would be safe; but in order to reach the cellar, we had to leave the house through the storefront and go around to the back of the house.

The words afraid or scared cannot convey the depths of our fear. Although we had been taught to always be respectful of whites, we were always a little wary of them. It wasn't until that day in 1921, that I realized just how much we were hated. It was devastating to my young mind to suddenly realize that we were not only hated because God made us a different color, but the white people wanted to kill all of us.

I was paralyzed with fear, too afraid to move and too afraid to stay where I was in front of the window. My mother screamed again. "Denise! We've got to leave here, honey!" I suddenly realized why we had to leave. We were being hunted like deer or rabbits in the woods. We were prey and the white people were the hunters. We had to leave because living depended on our getting away from the hunters.

I slowly backed away from the window and turned to follow my mother and sister through the darkened house. As we slowly moved down the steps and toward the front door, we held onto each other by the hand. Then something came crashing through the front window and the room was suddenly ablaze.

My mother pulled us toward the floor while she tried to keep us moving to the door. We couldn't see or breathe. Smoke filled our lungs and we all gasped and coughed. My mother's hand slipped from my grasp and suddenly I felt as if I were alone in the blazing house. I could smell the burning shoe polishes and dyes. I tried to feel my way to my mother but I couldn't feel or see my mother or sister. My fear leaped to new heights and I began to scream out but the smoke quickly choked my screams away. The walls, the floor and almost everything in the shop were on fire. I crawled toward the front door, feeling the skin of my hands and knees burning as I went.

I crawled over something in the floor and the thought that it was the body of my little sister gripped me with a new horror. My voice was suddenly resurrected and I screamed as loud as I could. Through my own screaming, I heard my father's voice calling me.

"Here! I'm here daddy," I said though I couldn't see him. Soon I felt his strong arms as he lifted me from the burning floor.

The next thing I knew, we were outside and moving between the two houses. The first thing I saw were dead bodies covering the sidewalks and in the middle of the street. People who had been set on fire were still burning and hanging from lamp post and signs. The carnage seemed unreal to me, as if I were having an endless nightmare though the heat from the fires that burned all around us was real enough.

Finally, we reached the cellar and my father opened the door. My mother was the first to climb down the rickety old wood steps. Then my father handed Frances down to my mother. After Fran, it was my turn. The steps were so steep that you had to go down them backward. I put one foot down and turned to grab hold of the railing. My father held onto my left arm to steady me. Then he was suddenly struck from behind and his body lurched forward letting go of my arm and almost falling into the cellar face forward.

My arms went forward instinctively to catch him though I was much too small to actually hold on to him. In a split second, he regained his balance and turned. He pulled his gun from his belt and quickly pulled the trigger twice. Two shots rang out and I heard, rather than saw, as the body of a man thudded to the ground. Then my father stumbled down the steps, closing the door to the cellar behind him.

I reached up to help him and as my arms went around his back, I felt a sticky saturation. At first I did not realize what it was as my mind was so traumatized. It took only moments, but I soon realized that the stickiness was blood. My father had been shot in the shoulder. Panic surged, flooding my brain and my body as I pulled my hand away from the wetness. "Help! Help! They shot daddy," I yelled. "He's bleeding! Oh God, Mommy! He's bleeding."

My mother was immediately by my side, pushing me away so she could get to my father. With mother's help, Daddy was able to climb down into the cellar. Mother secured the door with a piece of wood through the handle. The noise of the mob was somewhat muted in the cellar. The gunfire sounded far away now, as did the screams of the dying and wounded. The cellar smelled of wet soil and mold.

Blood soaked through my father's jacket as he stumbled down the stairs. My mother sat him on a barrel and helped him pull off his jacket and shirt.

"Denise," she yelled at me. "Look in those boxes and find something I can use to bandage your Daddy's shoulder." I went to the stack of boxes in the corner but as I went to open the first, I realized that the palms of my hands had been seriously burned. The fire had burned away the first layers of my skin, leaving my palms white and streaked with blood. I screamed as I looked down at them. My legs were also burned.

My mother rushed to my side. "Oh my God, Frank! Her hands and legs are burned!" My sister began to cry again.

My memory of what happened next is somewhat vague as the sight of my own wounds made me lose consciousness for a short time. I was aware that my mother was wrapping my hands and legs in torn pieces of fabric. She also bandaged my father's shoulder. All the while, the noise above us seemed to go on forever though it also seemed to move further and further away.

When finally there was quiet above, it was the middle of the night. My father roused us saying, "Come on, up with you," he whispered. "Get up now."

My mother sat up, her face held both shock and surprise. "Frank, what are you thinking?"

"I'm thinking that we best be getting out of here. We ain't got nothing to stay here for now."

My mother had always appeared to me to be so strong that there wasn't anything that she couldn't handle. For the first time in my short life, I knew that she was truly afraid and her fear infected us all. "What are we going to do? Where will we go, Frank?"

My father took her into his arms and tried to comfort her. "It will be all right, Marie. I promise." He kissed her cheek and held her close for only a minute. "Marie," he whispered against her head. "You know that there ain't no tellin what that white mob will do once its daylight again. We got to leave now, baby."

"Where, Frank? Where are we supposed to go?"

"I ain't got all the answers Marie, but if we hurry, I think we can make it to the Osage Hills before the sun comes up."

My mother did not protest further and we all prepared to leave the only home we kids had ever known. There was nothing to take with us except ourselves so we left the cellar quickly. As soon as we reached the street, the first thing that hit us was the sheer magnitude of the destruction. The entire block, over forty buildings, including our house, were burned to the ground. The smell of burned wood and flesh filled the air. The acrid air assaulted our senses but there was no time for complaining. My mother held Fran's hand and pulled her along. My father was ahead of us with me following close behind him. I kept my eyes on my parents. It may sound ridiculous now, but at that moment, I felt that if I took my eyes away from them, they would both perish in the madness that had besieged our small community.

As we moved further out of town and into the hills, the sun began to rise and the air became clearer but we were still suffering from the anxiety of the previous night. After we had walked for a while, Mother said we needed to rest and we all huddled together on the downside of a hill. As we lay there in the grass that was still moist from the morning dew, we all silently wondered what was next. The sky became busy with small aircraft gliding low over the hills. Behind us, there was still smoke emanating from the city. My father crawled on his belly to the top of the hill to see what was left of Greenwood.

He was gone less than five minutes when he scampered down to us to report that armed troops were ushering what was left of the men of our small community in orderly lines toward the center of town. "Come on," he said. "I'd be willing to bet that they will all be behind bars before the day's end. We've got to get out of here."

"But why," my mother protested. "They wouldn't arrest us. We didn't do anything."

"I bet half of them men they're marching down the road didn't do anything either."

My mother seemed to weigh this bit of information before she went on. "Were you able to speak with the sheriff?"

"No. We couldn't even get near the courthouse. By the time we were a block away, there was already a crowd. The closer we got the more rowdy the crowd became. Someone threw a bottle against the courthouse steps and the next thing we knew, we were running for our lives." He paused as if reflecting with new awareness. "Looks like we're still running for our lives."

"But where will we go?"

"Anywhere, let's just get as far away from Tulsa as we can."

Silently, we trudged on. It seemed as though we had been walking for days. In truth, it was only a couple of hours. An older white man approached us on horseback. The four of us just stopped and froze where we were. We didn't know whether to run or go toward him. "You from Greenwood?" the man asked.

"Yes sir," my father said with his head low, his eyes not daring to meet the blue eyes of this stranger.

"Yeah, well," the man said as he scratched at his bearded face. "I heard about the trouble over there in Greenwood."

My father didn't answer.

"Where you headed?" the man asked.

"Hominy," Daddy said. "I got family over in Hominy."

The old man chuckled. "Are you planning to walk all the way there?"

"Look Mister," my father said, losing his patience and lifting his head in defiance. "We don't mean anybody any harm. I just want to get my family away from the trouble in Tulsa."

The man jumped down from his horse and walked toward my father. Daddy stood where he was but the rest of us backed away. It was clear that this man wasn't part of the mob that had attacked Greenwood but he was a white man, and by then we didn't know who to trust. "Well, I don't blame you but far as I can tell, you'd be walkin a mighty distance to get to Hominy. Besides," he chuckled again. "You're going in the wrong direction. Hominy is due west," he pointed as he spoke. "I got my truck over at the house. I'd be willing to give you a lift if you like?" he smiled and we all let out a sigh of relief.

"I'd be much obliged," Daddy said.

"You all wait here. I'll be back with my truck in a few minutes."

To this day, I remember that man and his kindly old face. His name was Mr. Tucker. We all piled into the back of his pickup and he and my Daddy talked about what was going on in Tulsa. Mr. Tucker said that he'd read in the morning paper that over four blocks had been burned and three hundred people killed. He didn't care what started the riot, he just thought it was a shame that it led to such ugliness. We later learned that the KKK had attacked and bombed Greenwood on the same day we left town.

It took some time but in Hominy, my parents had to start all over again. At first, we stayed with my father's cousin in a big old farm house. My father helped around the farm and his cousin, who we called Uncle Ron, let Daddy use a small plot of land to grow tomatoes, collards, and peppers in their season. He took his crops to town and sold them at a roadside stand. In three years, he saved enough money to open another shoe repair shop in Hominy.

We had lived through one of the worst race riots in American History and I know that it changed all of us in one way or another. Of one thing, I am certain; none of us will ever forget the day Little Africa burned.

This story is a fictional account of the 1921 Tulsa, Oklahoma Race Riots. If you'd like to read more about this event that was omitted of U.S. History books, go to http://www.cnn.com/US/9908/03/tulsa.riots.probe.

WHEN SNOWFLAKES FALL

The sun was warm, a silent promise of spring's early arrival. A cool breeze fluttered through the artificial vales made by tall city buildings as if winter was not ready to take her final breath.

Bree took off her jacket and slowed her pace, reveling in the unexpected pleasant weather. It was somewhat easier to be inside in the stoic atmosphere of an office building during the cold, dark days of winter, she thought. Today the sun beckoned to her. Spring was definitely in the air and Bree inhaled the heady aroma of the coming season, letting her spirit rise as if the dawn of a new season offered the promise of new possibilities.

As she moved slowly down Spruce Street, contemplating blowing off the rest of the day, she noticed that some of the businesses she passed had propped open their doors and sidewalk cafes were hosing down outdoor furniture. In small patches where the concrete had been cut away, tulip buds were pushing through the soil. When Bree came to the small city park where she had planned to eat a quick lunch and scan the daily paper, it was evident that she wasn't the only one with spring fever, as the park was alive with people.

She waded through the throngs of people until she found an empty bench. After she had eaten her lunch, scanned the newspaper and abandoned her plans to blow off the day, she gathered her things and prepared to return to the office.

"May I share your bench?" It was a robust baritone voice that spoke to her.

"Yes, of course," Bree said as she looked up at the tall well-dressed man.

"Thank you." His ascent was unusual. It was English but not American or British. Maybe Australian, she thought.

"Do we know each other?" Bree asked though she knew she had no recollection of being in the presence of this handsome man before that moment. She smiled to herself, silently admitting that she wanted no more than to hear him speak again.

His smile was broad. His teeth were straight and white. "We have not been formally introduced but we have crossed paths on occasion." There was music in his voice, a rich melody, deep and provocative. Now Bree was even surer that they had never met because she knew that she would have remembered this man. "My name is Shombay," he said as he presented his perfectly manicured hand.

They shook hands. His touch was gentle. "My name is Bree," she said.

"I am pleased to meet you Bree."

"Likewise; the bench is all yours," she said as she pushed her bag onto her shoulder and stood to leave. Their eyes met for only a second but the moment seemed to distend time as she inhaled the essence of this man. "Where," she muttered awkwardly.

"Excuse me?"

"You said that our paths have crossed. I don't remember seeing you before."

He smiled again. "We both work in the Witherspoon Building. I have seen you from time to time."

"Oh," Bree tried to sound nonchalant. The truth was there was something about this man that touched her. It was more than his good looks and his accent. "Well, you have a nice afternoon."

"You also," he said.

Bree turned and walked away. The urge to turn around and take just one more glance was overwhelming. After she put a few yard of distance between them, she gave in to her urge and turned to find him watching her as she walked away. Even in the space between them, his dark eyes held her captive. She waived and he waived back.

It would be weeks before they saw each other again but Bree could think of little else. She found herself thinking of him day and night. Though she could not name it or explain it away, there was something about Shombay that was enticing. Bree could hardly deny that she wanted more than anything to know this man. He was probably between thirty and thirty-five and the tailored suit was an indication that he was a professional. She tried to think of all the businesses in building, wondering just where he worked and where their paths may have crossed.

Bree worked as a paralegal for a small law firm. Two weeks after their meeting in the park, Shombay came to her office and asked her out to dinner. He looked as tall and handsome as she remembered and his mere presence rendered Bree speechless for a moment. She nodded her acceptance to the dinner invitation, still in complete awe of the man that stood before her.

That first dinner led to many others and they soon became a couple. Among the usual revelations of a new relationship, Bree learned that Shombay was Nigerian. His family had migrated to the states when he was eighteen. His parents were both doctors. He had done his undergrad and graduate studies at Temple University and was now a law clerk in one of Philadelphia's most prestigious law firms while he studied to take the bar exam.

Over the next few weeks, their budding relationship blossomed into a bouquet of emotion, desire, and passion. Together they seemed to move in time with the rhythm of the earth and the new season. Their relationship progressed quickly as Shombay was the most attentive and thoughtful man Bree had ever dated.

So many of the men she'd dated since college were lacking in one way or another. Some were too close to their mothers and others wanted to be too close to Bree. The boy she had dated during the last year of high school and the beginning of college had ended their three-year relationship suddenly and without explanation. The breakup was devastating to Bree and left her guarded and distrustful of men. She erected emotional barriers around her wounded heart as a way of protecting herself from the emotional wounds of another failed love.

But Shombay was different and their connection to each other was different. He somehow managed to slip around all the walls that barricaded Bree's heart. He listened to her and she found herself telling him things about herself and her life that she would never have told another sole. He showered her with compliments and gifts. They weren't expensive gifts, just little things that told her that he thought of her even when they weren't together. He sent her flowers with little love notes on the card. He sometimes called her in the middle of the day just to say that he was thinking about her. Bree didn't even know that she had removed those long placed barriers and completely opened her heart to Shombay.

Their love-making was passionate and mutually satisfying. Attentive, caring, and educated, Shombay seemed to be all that any woman could want in a man. When they weren't out on a date, their time was divided between their respective apartments.

Bree knew that she was falling in love. "It's too soon," she told herself, while at the same time she knew that she could do nothing to stop the fire that burned in her heart and the love that was steadily growing for this man. She only hoped that Shombay shared her feelings. That was the spring of their relationship.

By the time the sun blazed over Philadelphia and summer was in full swing, the two were inseparable. Longtime friends were pushed to the wayside as Shombay occupied more and more of Bree's time. He took her to meet his family and they received her well. She took him to meet her family and although her father and brother had some reservations about him, they received him well enough. Her brother wanted to know if Shombay's culture allowed him to have more than one wife.

Bree quickly dismissed this notion, though she and Shombay had never discussed the topic. "He not a Muslim," Bree explained. "Besides, we're just dating. We haven't even thought of marriage."

Eventually, Bree began to spend more time in Shombay's apartment than her own. One warm summer evening as they dined on the balcony of his Lafayette Hills apartment, Shombay said that it was senseless for them to both be paying rent when she spent so much time in his apartment. He suggested that Bree give up her Rittenhouse apartment and move in with him.

"That's a pretty big step, Shombay. I'm not sure I'm ready for us to live together."

"We're practically living together already. I love you, Bree. I want to spend every moment that I can with you. I want to spend the rest of my life with you. Why do you see something wrong in that?"

"I don't and I love you too. It's just that . . . ," she paused to make sure she would speak just the right words. She believed in his love and his devotion to her, but his appeal seemed to be lacking in some way. "Marriage," the unspoken word hung in the air like a piñata filled with all of the hopes and dreams of her future. If Shombay truly wanted to spend the rest of his life with her, why was he not offering his hand in marriage?

Her mind raced ahead and backward at the same time and whirled with unspoken questions. Had she missed some clue? Had she not gone into this relationship with her eyes wide open? How could she have known that she would fall so deeply in love with a man who did not share those precious feelings? She had shared her hopes, dreams and ambitions with this man. Could he not see that living together would be contrary to everything she believed in? Should she even bring up the subject or would he think that she was somehow trying to manipulate him into a marriage that he obviously had not considered? "I feel like I'd be giving up my independence if I left my own apartment," she finally said.

"So you're saying that having your own apartment makes you independent?" His tone was stern. It was a tone that she had not previously heard from Shombay. He gave her a sidelong glance.

"No. I'm just not sure that I'm ready for that step in our relationship. We've only known each other for such a short time."

"I see," he seemed to weigh her answer then he smiled. Bree couldn't quite understand the smile until she realized that it wasn't a smile at all. It was a smirk. He looked at her as if her opinion in this matter was ridiculous and not worthy of a rebuttal.

There was no more talk of them moving in together. That conversation marked the beginning of a change in their relationship. He was the same man of course, but Bree had begun to notice subtle changes in Shombay's demeanor. At times, he was distant as if his mind was someplace else. The attention that she came to expect from him seemed sometimes trite, as if he were indulging a spoiled child. She decided that it might be best if she just pulled back a little, give them both time to reevaluate their relationship.

Bree made an effort to rebuild the friendships she had neglected in favor of her relationship with Shombay. She called old girl friends and even some male friends. Some of her girlfriends were unforgiving for the most part, reminding her that she hadn't wanted their company a few months ago. "I guess I deserve that," Bree said to Sharon, the only friend that seemed to understand what she was going through.

"Damn right you deserve it! You just dropped us like you couldn't be so bothered."

"All right, all right, I admit it, but you know that if you'd met a man that you thought was going to be the love of your life, you would have dropped me just as fast and hard."

"Damn right?" Sharon said again and they both laughed. They made plans to have dinner together that evening. Bree told Sharon of the excitement she'd felt when she and Shombay first met, her misgivings about moving in together and the sudden distantness he now displayed. Sharon not only offered advice, she allowed Bree to unburden her heart.

It felt good being out with her girlfriend. Bree had almost forgotten what sisterhood felt like. They laughed and talked the night away. After dinner, they went to a movie and on the way home; they stopped at a little South Street club for a few drinks before going home. It was close to one in the morning when Sharon dropped Bree off at her apartment. She was tired but in very good spirits as she and her friend had enjoyed a great night out.

As she fished in her purse for her key, she was still humming to the tune of Alicia's Keys new record, which had been playing at the club when they left. She entered the lobby of her apartment building, unaware that someone had been waiting for her arrival. It wasn't until she walked to the elevators and pushed the up button that she saw Shombay standing in the shadow, partially hidden by a large potted plant.

"Shombay?" she asked surprised.

In two long strides, he was at her side and with one hand, he gripped her by the elbow and proceeded to usher her into the elevator. Bree pulled away from his grasp.

"What the hell is wrong with you?" she said.

"Me?" His anger was etched in the lines of his forehead. "I would ask you what the hell is wrong with you.

Have you completely forgotten yourself? A lady does not come home at one in the morning with alcohol on her breath. Where were you?"

Bree just looked at him. At first, she was astonished but her astonishment quickly turned to amusement, no doubt the few glasses of Merlot she'd consumed accounted for some of the amusement. She smiled at him and then laughed outright as she leaned back against the elevator wall as it slowly climbed to the tenth floor. The bell sounded signaling that the elevator at reached the designated floor. When the doors opened, Bree slowly walked pass Shombay and didn't bother to answer his repeated questions. "Where were you, Bree? Are you seeing someone else? I want to know who you were out with!" Shombay demanded. "You aren't even going to give me an answer, are you?" he said as he followed her to her apartment door.

"No!" she said. "I am an adult woman and as such I am not obligated to answer to anyone, least of all you."

"But you are my woman," he said.

Bree opened the door then turned to face him. "Exactly," she said. "I am your woman, not your child. Now if you don't mind, I'm tired. It's been a long day. Good night Shombay." With that, she slide inside the door and quickly closed it behind her leaving a confused Shombay starring at the closed door.

It was several weeks before Bree heard from Shombay again. Summer was winding down and fall loomed ahead. They'd planned to take a one day cruise down the Delaware River on Labor Day but he didn't call and she refused to call him. When he finally called a week later, it appeared that all was forgiven. There was no mention of sharing apartments or questioning her about whom she saw or where she'd been. It seemed that the Shombay she had fallen in love with was back.

Their relationship resumed almost as if there hadn't been a break on his part, but for Bree the break had made her realize that to build her life around this man, any man, was a mistake.

They did see each other regularly but she also made time for her friends. It became obvious to Bree that every time she made plans to spend time with friends, even those occasions when the two of them went out with friends together, Shombay was less than enthusiastic. He would sometimes sulk and make excuses not to be included. He wanted Bree all to himself.

By the time fall came and the days became shorter and nights were chilly, Bree and Shombay seemed to be once again comfortable with each other. They still made passionate love, still cared deeply for one another but something had changed. Whatever it was that wilted with their disagreement over living together, it had not been revived. Neither was willing to articulate this new relationship but they both sensed it. This unnamed thing between them seemed to grow like a stain, an imperfection that began to pull at the fragile bond of their new relationship. Bree silently refused to devote herself entirely to Shombay and he was suspicious and uncomfortable with a woman that he could not control.

Ignoring their perspective misgivings, they forged on together. They took long road trips through the Lehigh Valley to admire the changing colors of the rich foliage of Western Pennsylvania. They even spent a weekend in the Pocono Mountains.

When he told her in January that he would be traveling back to Nigeria with his parents for a couple of weeks, she did not think anything was amiss.

It was a cold January Saturday and Bree awoke to the sound of the television. The local news was predicting a fierce winter storm moving up the east coast. Bree sleepily sat up to pay closer attention. Shombay was busy packing and preparing for his trip. "Wow," she said. "If this storm is as bad as they're saying, you might not be able to get a flight out of Philadelphia tomorrow."

At first Shombay didn't answer. Bree thought he hadn't heard her. "Honey, this storm seems like it's going to be a really bad one."

"I must go," he said emphatically.

"Well, what will you do if the planes are not flying? If the weather is too bad the airport will ground the plans."

"I will find a way. Please do not concern yourself with my affairs." His stern tone was back and Bree couldn't understand what she had done to upset him. Without another word, Bree got up, took a shower, and dressed quickly. She was intent on returning to her own apartment and leaving Shombay and his foul attitude to himself. As soon as he noticed that she was leaving, he became enraged. "Where are you going?" he yelled.

"I'm going back to my own apartment before this storm makes it so I'm stuck here with you and your bad attitude."

"Well go then, if that is what pleases you!"

Her coat hung in a small closet in his entry hall. Bree swung open the door and pulled her coat from the hanger. In her haste, she accidentally knocked a large envelope from the top shelve of the closet. It fell to the floor, its contents spilling out at her feet. There were several hand written letters, his passport and a photo of two young African women and several children. Of course, they must be family.

When Shombay came into the living room and saw Bree picking up the envelope's contents from the floor, he charged at her. "What the hell are you doing? Are you so insecure that you would rifle through my personal belongings?" He snatched the photo and the envelope from her hand.

"I wasn't snooping Shombay. I accidentally knocked the envelope down." Bree wondered why he was so upset. "What is it? What has got you so worked up?"

"Nothing!" He was looking down at the photo.

"Is there something wrong with your family?" Bree asked with genuine concern. She suddenly didn't care that he'd been in a bad mood all morning. She only wanted to console him if she could. "What is it, Shombay?"

"It is not your problem Bree."

With that, she started just walking out of the door, but he called her back. "Bree," he walked to the sofa and sat down. "There is something that I must tell you."

Bree went back into the apartment and stood in front of Shombay. She didn't say anything. She just waited for him to speak. He handed her the photo. She looked down at the two women in brightly colored dresses and then back to Shombay.

"They are my wives and my children," he said.

Bree just stood there as if she hadn't heard what he said. Silent moments passed as his words penetrated her consciousness. Her first thought was that her brother had been right about Shombay. The image of Shombay, who sat with his head in his hands as if he had been wounded, repulsed her. She realized that besides her initial attraction, their relationship had always been about Shombay. Had this happened months ago, she would have felt as if she had just been punched in the stomach; but it didn't happen months ago. Tears welled in her eyes but she did not cry out. "Why didn't you tell me that you were married? How could you do this? How could your parents treat me with such kindness if they knew that you were married?"

"It is not as complicated as it seems. I came here for my education. My parents and I knew that I would return to my country eventually but I am a man. I have needs. I am away from my family for months, sometimes years at a time."

"So, you used me just to satisfy your needs? Is that what I am to you?" Even as she uttered those words, she knew the answer that he would not be man enough to admit.

Shombay stood up and went to Bree, but she backed away from him. "Don't be so melodramatic Bree. Of course you mean more to me but your fierce desire for independence makes you unsuitable as a wife."

"I'm not suitable as a wife," she repeated. "You're right Shombay, I am not suitable to be one of a collection of wives." She waited for him to respond but he just stood there looking down on her. "So are you admitting that our entire relationship was some kind of test to see if I were suitable? Don't answer that, we both already know the answer. Shombay, I have no desire to be one of your wives." Bree turned to leave.

"No, Bree, don't leave. I don't want you to be upset with me. Please sit, let us talk this out."

"There is nothing to talk out Shombay. You lied to me and you used me."

"Please forgive me. I will be back in a month and I would like very much to see you when I return."

Bree smiled up at him. "I don't think so Shombay."

"Why do you smile while your lips say no?"

"Oh, I don't know. Maybe it's because I really thought that you were an honorable man and right now, all I see is your arrogance. The fact that you believe that you can use me, lie to me, and expect me to be here waiting for your return is laughable. I hope your family is well and I wish you all the happiness and success in the world."

"And, what about you?"

"I'll be all right. Please don't worry about me." Her sarcasm went unnoticed. "Goodbye Shombay. I'll never forget you." She moved through the doorway, quickly closing it behind her." She waited in the corridor for a few moments to see if he would come after her, and when he didn't; she knew that it was finally over.

The storm did come as predicted. It started late Saturday afternoon and snowed all through the night. Alone in her apartment with a bottle of her favorite wine and with jazz softly wafting through the apartment, Bree let her mind travel back over the time she'd spent with Shombay. The spring of their relationship had been good, better than good. By fall, the blooming relationship had come to the end of its season and begun to wilt. Now it was winter and the relationship was dead. After the initial shock, she realized that she really wasn't as hurt as she expected. Maybe she always knew that he was hiding something and she was just waiting for the other shoe to drop, as they say.

She lay back on the pillows she had propped up in front of the stereo and closed her eyes. In her mind's eye, she could see Shombay as he was that first day in the park. He stood in front of her with his perfectly tailored gray suit, his coffee bean complexion, wide sensuous smile and perfect white teeth. He was fine and Bree knew that if she'd had to do it all again she would have easily. She acknowledged that Shombay was wrong for not telling her about his family and a part of her hated him for his lying but she didn't really hate him. She felt that hate was too strong a word for someone she once loved. It was just another chapter in her life that was now closed. She would move on and love would eventually come again but she would always think of Shombay and their short love affair whenever snowflakes fall.

KARMA

Richard slide one of his arms from under the warmth of down filled comforter, stretching to hit the snooze button on his clock radio. A minute later he rolled out of bed and shut off the alarm altogether. He stretched and yawned, willing himself alert. His bare feet sunk into the pile of the rich carpet as he stumbled toward the bathroom. Women's clothes flung on the arm chair in the corner reminded him that he had not been alone the night before.

He glanced back at the bed, the figure was complete covered, and Richard couldn't for the life of him, remember what her name was or even if she were black or white. He detoured from his bathroom destination to uncover his overnight guest. He grabbed the covers and threw them back. The sudden rush of cool air awoke the sleeping woman and she sat up. "Oh, Peggy," Richard said.

"Megan," she corrected.

"Whatever," he said.

Megan pushed her tousled blond hair from her eyes. "How about some breakfast?" she asked.

"I don't think so," Richard retorted. "How about we do this another time?"

"You mean you want me to leave?" a surprised Megan said.

"The night is over, honey. That means the date is over too." Richard smiled at the look of shock that registered on Megan's face.

"Why so rude?"

"Oh, was I rude? Sorry."

"Can I at least take a shower?"

"Sure you can. You do have a shower in your apartment, don't you?"

With that, Megan bolted from the bed and began to dress. "Funny, you didn't seem like such a jerk last night," she said as she grabbed her purse and jacket and headed for the door.

"Last night I wanted you. This morning, I just want to be rid of you," Richard said as he slammed the door behind her.

Once he was alone, he took a shower and prepared for his morning meeting downtown.

Richard checked his reflection in the mirror once last time before leaving his apartment. He smiled, appreciating the successful look of the man that stared back at him. His Armani suit, tailored to fit his well-toned physique, was an emblem of his achievements in the world of business. Richard appreciated the finer things of life. The silk tie with matching handkerchief for his breast pocket, the sharp haircut, and splash of Aramis, and shoes shined to a brilliant gleam, told the world that this was a man who recognized the value of a good living. He smiled at his reflection and stopped short of blowing himself a kiss.

Richard exuded charm and good looks, which stood him well in many of his business relationships, but he was also cunning and dishonest. The charm was little more than a veneer used to get whatever he wanted. He had long ago adopted the edict that all was fair in business. His knack for appearing to be charming allowed him to get close to people who would never suspect that he held any ill-fated motives against them, but Richard was a man of very little regard for his fellowman. If people were somehow duped by his dishonesty, he thought them of little account to be taken so easily. It was all a game to Richard and he refused to lose on any level.

The doorman, an old black man, probably in his sixties, had smiled at Richard as he left the building. "Good morning Mr. Davis," he'd said. Richard had only nodded in affirmation as if this man was unworthy of a spoken word. Richard pulled is new Cadillac Escalade out of the parking lot of his Bala Cynwyd Apartment building. He had plenty of time before his 10:00 a.m. meeting and Richard prided himself on being prompt. He'd take the drive into center city and be there in time to grab a cup of coffee and peruse the morning paper. However, the drive was backed up for miles. Traffic was at a complete stand still from the Falls Bridge forward.

Richard shifted uneasily in his seat, his frustration mounting. This was an important meeting and he really didn't want to be late. As traffic inched forward at a snail's pace, Richard found himself thinking about his life before success. He thought of old man Harry Ling. That had been where it all began.

Richard and his best friend Tony had started their first business renovating fifty-year-old row homes of Philadelphia. They called their new business, Davis and Harris Renovations. Richard and Tony made a good team and they were good at what they did. Their reputation for doing renovations efficiently and timely was spread by word of mouth and in the first six months, they had enough work to spread throughout the year and beyond. That's when they were contacted by Harry Ling.

Mr. Ling was a Korean American who owed a neighborhood gym in an old run down warehouse. He wanted to turn his place into a real state of the art gym, with showers, lockers and an indoor Jacuzzi. Both Richard and Tony were excited about the new job but Richard was more than excited. He took one look at that gym and suddenly he had a vision of the new gym. The only difference was that he saw himself as the owner and not Mr. Ling.

Richard and Tony agreed to do the job and Richard went to his attorney for the written agreement. This agreement was different from any he had previously negotiated. He had his lawyer add a clause that stated that if Mr. Ling was more than thirty days late on any payment, the property would be ceased as payment for the entire amount of money owed. Richard knew that Mr. Ling had gambled his entire life savings on the business of his dreams. Richard also knew that Tony would never agree to such an agreement, which is why he took great care to keep his plan a secret for as long as possible. Tony believed that being honest and patient with their customers made good business sense.

It took six months to renovate the gym and it was less than a year later when Mr. Ling defaulted on his payments. Richard wasted no time in ceasing the property. Mr. Ling threatened to sue but no attorney would touch the case because Mr. Ling had signed the agreement.

Richard and Tony argued vehemently about Richard's unscrupulous business practices. "Why do you care so much about what happens to Ling?" Richard said.

"It just isn't Ling, and you know it," Tony argued.

"Look Tony," Richard placed his hand on Tony's shoulder as he spoke. "I care as much about Mr. Ling as they cared about us when they bought up all the small businesses in our old neighborhood."

"Don't talk to me like I'm stupid. This has nothing to do with race. You wanted that gym even before we finished the renovations," Tony said. When the argument ended so did their partnership and friendship. The business was dissolved.

This was the first of Richard's acquisitions. Acquiring that gym had been so easy that Richard now developed a thirst for expansion. He opened a telemarketing business, a string of day care centers, and used car lots. Davis and Harris

Renovations became Davis Enterprises. He owned and rented properties throughout Philadelphia.

The world saw Richard as a self-made man, a black man with little education but unencumbered ambition who had made it. He even won the Businessman of the Year Award for 2003. Those who had dealt with Richard knew him as a pariah. He had made his fortune on the backs of many who had trusted and admired him. Richard had no regrets, no sleepless nights, or pangs of sympathy for those he had ruined in his rise to prominence. The thought brought a smile to his face as he told himself that it had all been worth it.

Finally, the traffic had inched forward and Richard found himself at the crossing of the Strawberry Mansion Bridge. He pulled to the right and his escalade climbed the hill with ease. Another right and he was speeding through the park. He turned off on Lancaster Avenue and headed east, toward the center of the city. This was the heart of West Philadelphia, the old neighborhood.

As he speed past the little streets that branched to and from the avenue, Richard again though of the past. He thought of Laura and the son they'd had together. They were both in high school when Laura became pregnant. Laura had been accepted on an academic scholarship to Howard University while Richard had made no plans for his life after high school. At first, Richard was proud that he would become a father but as the reality of their situation became clear, he decided that he didn't want to be a father. When he suggested that Laura abort the child, reminding her that her college plans would have to be postponed indefinitely, she was outraged. Their relationship ended on that day and Richard never looked back. Eight months later, he received a card, which had been mailed to his mother's residence, stating that Laura had delivered a healthy baby boy. Richard never contacted Laura, never saw his son, and never heard from her again. He hadn't thought of Laura in years. He now wondered what had become of Laura and his son.

On this blustery November morning, a constant dribble of cold rain and wind swept wet leaves whirled across the wet sidewalks of center city Philadelphia. Richard pulled into the parking lot under Liberty Place and took the elevator to the eleventh floor.

He strode into the conference room with his usual confidence. The long table was lined with men in business suites on both sides, and at the head was a young woman who Richard did not immediately recognize. According to his schedule, this was a meeting with the board of directors of an investment company he was attempting to buy but something in the demeanor of the men sitting at the table gave Richard a moment of pause. These men did not have the look of investment bankers. Their suits were common, probably bought from a department store. In fact, Richard felt almost over dressed as he entered the room and took his seat among them. He uttered a soft, "good morning," as he looked from face to face.

"Good morning Mr. Davis," the woman said. "I know that you expected this to be a meeting to iron out the details of your acquisition of Bearston and Wakefield Investments, however, we are prepared to offer you a more substantial deal." Richard nodded, suddenly unsure of the real purpose of this meeting.

"Let me introduce you to the gentlemen who will be negotiating this agreement," the woman said.

"Starting from your left, this is Mr. Clarkson, of the city License and Inspection Department. Next is Mr. Braxton, head of the state Free Trade Commission." The woman paused to see if Richard was the slightest bit aware of what was happening and he gave no indication that he was aware. "Next to Mr. Braxton," the woman went on. "I'm sure you already know Mr. Anthony Harris."

That's when it finally struck Richard that this meeting was something very different from what he had expected. "Wait a minute!" Richard said as he pushed his chair back and stood up. "What the hell is going on here?"

"I suggest that you take your seat Mr. Davis," the woman said and Richard swung around to face her. His expression melted away like the wax of a burning candle as recognition of the woman came to him. It was Laura. She wasn't the pretty little cheerleader he'd talked into losing her virginity in the basement of his parent's home. He then turned his attention to Tony, who didn't look at all like the naive boy who thought that treating people well was a profitable business practice. As his gaze moved down the long table, he saw many faces that he recognized, including Mr. Ling. "What the hell is going on here?" he asked again.

Laura handed Richard a sheet of paper on which were a list of charges concerning his unlawful business practices. Richard scanned the list and then threw the paper into the center of the table. "Oh, I see. You all want to take me down. You're all jealous because none of you had the nerve or the business sense to be prosperous. You all want to blame me for your failings."

"You're wrong, as usual," said Tony.

"You have not been charged with anything, Mr. Davis," Laura said. "That paper is a list of both city and state violations for which you could be charged, if I have a mind to do so. In addition, I assure you the charges would stick. We have amassed enough evidence against you to, not only ruin your enterprise, but to put you behind bars for a considerable length of time. However, that is not our wish. You have cheated, stolen from or swindled almost everyone in this room and what we want is reparations. We want you to pay us for what you have taken from all of us." She handed him another sheet of paper. "I think this would satisfy us."

Richard took the page and scanned the list. "I can't pay you this." His outrage was clearly written on his face. "I'd be ruined! You can't expect me to pay this."

"That is exactly what we want," said Mr. Ling. "You're a resourceful guy. I'm sure you'll bounce back."

"You don't really have a choice in this Mr. Davis," said another.

"Who the hell are you?" Richard wanted to know.

"My name is Mr. Benson. I am the assistant district attorney."

"You see," Laura added. "If you don't sign this agreement to pay us exactly what you stole from us, we will file these charges before the end of the day. It's your call. Pay us or take your chance in the court."

The room became very quiet as Richard contemplated his situation. He knew of the crimes he had committed, the people he'd hurt on the way up and he also knew that in a court of law the chances that he would be convicted were great. His back was against the wall. Everything that he had done to make it to the top was now falling down upon him. If he did nothing, he knew he would surely be crushed. He lifted his head and looked at the faces of the men around the table. Their faces held the smirk of victory, which had so often belonged to him. He smiled to himself with the thought that their victory would be hollow. When his eyes landed on Laura, she pushed the agreement along with a pen across the table to him. He took the agreement and hastily scrawled his signature before pushing it back to her. Why was she here, he wondered. He hadn't ever taken anything from Laura.

"Thank you Mr. Davis," Laura said as she gathered the papers and pushed them into her briefcase. The men at the table followed suit and they each stood and prepared to leave.

One by one they filed pass Richard, some patting him on the shoulder as they passed. Finally, there was only Laura, Richard, and Tony in the room. "What did I ever take from you?" Richard asked Laura.

"Nothing," Laura said with a smile. "If you thought you took my youth or my chance for an education when you abandoned me and your son, you couldn't be more wrong." She stood over Richard and smiled down at him. "I'm stronger than I look, Richard. Of course, I couldn't go away to school as I'd planned but I went to school right here in Philadelphia. I got a good education and for six years I raised my son alone."

"I guess you want me give you money now and come around to see you and the kid."

Laura gave a little laugh.

"Look Laura, I had plans. You and the kid just didn't fit into my plans."

Laura smiled again, broad and wide. "Well, things certainly have changed, haven't they?"

"What do you mean?"

"I don't want your money Richard. I am a very successful attorney. I don't even want you to come around and see my son, whose name is Tyrie. You had your chance to be a father to Tyrie fourteen years ago and you let us know that you couldn't handle the job. We did just fine on our own and now Tyrie has a new father."

Richard shrugged his shoulders with an 'I don't care,' flare. "Great," he said. "That's just great."

"More than you will ever know," Tony said as he slid his arm around Laura's slim waist. "The thing that you could never understand Richard was that what goes around eventually comes around. You've lived your entire life taking advantage of people. It was only a matter of time before the tables would be turned on you." The two strode from the room arm in arm, leaving Richard stunned with the realization that his once best friend was now father to his son and husband to his first love.

One would think that Richard learned a valuable lesson with the golden rule acted out in real life for him to see and comprehend. However, men like Richard are never receptive of such morality. What Richard learned was to be more careful the next time around.

OTHER WRITINGS BY
F. HAYWOOD GLENN

The Vance Legacy

A Novel

This is an unforgettable story of a family destroyed by secrets and lies. The story details the consequences that ensue when a thirty-year-old lie comes to light, revealing a dangerous family secret.
Passionate love and burning hatred move this emotionally charged story with devastating results. This is an American story of love and loss.

Dark Legacy

A Novel

This is the long-awaited sequel to The Vance Legacy and Big Bill's Legacy continues. Life in Philadelphia means freedom for Lillian and Rebecca, and a new love for Beth. A gripping and unforgettable page-turner. Three women are bound together by shared loss. They must learn to lean on each other as they forge new lives in Philadelphia.